Shipwrecked Body

Ana Clavel

translated from the Spanish by Jay Miskowiec

translation edited by Juan Arciniega

ALIFORM PUBLISHING

MINNEAPOLIS · OAXACA

ALIFORM PUBLISHING
is part of The Aliform Group
117 Warwick Street SE/Minneapolis, MN USA 55414
information@aliformgroup.com www.aliformgroup.com

Originally published in Mexico as *Cuerpo náufrago* by Alfaguara

Copyright © Aguilar, Altea, Taurus, Alfaguara, SA de CV, 2005

English translation copyright © Aliform Publishing, 2008

First published in the United States of America by
Aliform Publishing, 2008

La presente traducción fue realizada con apoyo del Programa de
Apoyo a la Traducción de Obras Mexicanas a Lenguas Extranjeras
(El ProTrad).

This publication was made possible with a generous grant from
the Programa de Apoyo a la Traducción de Obras Mexicanas en
Lenguas Extranjeras (ProTrad) of the Fondo Nacional para la
Cultura y las Artes of Mexico.

Library of Congress Control Number 2008926830

ISBN 978-0-9817072-0-4
ISBN 0-9817072-0-3

Set in Times New Roman

Shipwrecked Body

Ana Clavel

Table of Contents

*The answer has no memory,
only the question remembers.*

— Edmond Jabès

From One Body to Another

1

She—because there was no doubt about her sex, although the stressful times contributed to her assuming other roles—was asleep in bed, reluctant to abandon her last dream where three little boys ran out from class and at a signal took out their nascent penises in order to measure their prowess. She—whom we will shortly come to know as Antonia—watched the scene from each boy's point of view, finally settling on a kid still hiding his sex behind his hand. Seeing the size of the other members, he fearlessly showed his little larva. The sound of a school bell, or rather the alarm clock, prodded the boys towards a desperate maneuver: they jumped up to some ropes hanging from the ceiling and swung in a whirlwind of emanating light. Little Antonia, with her sex hanging down, sensed an oppressive force that took hold of the rope and made it tremble. The alarm kept insisting: Antonia the adult tried to hang onto the rope, but getting in sync with the other children had already become impossible. She reached toward the nightstand and instinctively made out the digital clock: 7:45. She hit the sleep button and went back to her pillow, but the little boys were already gone. In their place some bits of information fell into order: the meeting with the institute's PR director, an overdue phone bill, her gynecologist appointment. And the clothes she had to wear; a parade of blouses, tailored suits, nylons and high heels began to alternate in a dizzying fashion show of invisible models, models that suddenly hung from ropes knotted with unknown strength and suspended from the ceiling. Antonia opened her eyes and remembered the little boys. She frowned and murmured, "What a strange dream," passing her gaze over the ceiling where a translucent lamp hung indifferently, like the PR director's face as he listened to the weekly report. She had to hurry or she'd be late. She jumped from bed and ran towards the bathroom. On her way out of the bedroom she caught a glimpse of a puzzling figure in the full-length mirror she went past, forcing her to go back. Standing before the mirror she rubbed her eyes repeatedly. She must have been sleepwalking and was still dreaming. The boy in the dream was now a man. She herself, but at the same time undoubtedly a man: there between her legs, planted like an irreducible sign, was her new sex.

2

Misunderstandings begin with appearances. Are we what we appear to be? Does identity begin with what we see? And what was it that Antonia saw when she jumped out of bed and discovered herself in the mirror? The body of her desire. Then perhaps we'd have to admit that we were wrong: identity begins with what we desire. Secret, persistent, irrevocable. That which in reality desires us.

Well, if what had happened to her wasn't a dream, if beyond the mystery of the penis her back had become a bit broader, if the hair on her arms and legs, which she'd always had more of than most women, had gotten thicker, if her jaw had turned a little squarer and an Adam's apple hung slightly but undeniably from her throat…

She stood there for hours facing the mirror. At first she remained in a state of marvelous perplexity where she didn't even dare test those changes with her hands. The only thing running over her transformed body again and again were her eyes. Not that before Antonia hadn't enjoyed her body of a twenty-seven-year-old woman (she especially liked her small, rounded breasts and strong but shapely legs); rather she was astonished by the fragile boundary of differences, how a bit more tension, a curve less accentuated, a swelling hanging like a lead weight, could tip the balance.

And after the initial amazement came the questions. The truth of the matter is that ever since childhood she had wanted to be a man, not because she felt herself a man trapped in a woman's body, but because she was intrigued by the nature of those beings that, she supposed, were more fulfilled and freer than she was. Yes, she remembered perfectly how as a little girl she'd envied her brothers and their friends, their way of taking over a street for a soccer game, of going through the city with no big worry, of getting their hands and pants greasy tightening a bike chain, or wearing a suit and feeling important. More than once as a teenager she had dressed up in her bedroom, slicking back her hair and trying on her brothers' clothes. During those moments she felt as if she were descending to the depths of herself: a warm, dark zone like a cave where nothing was defined. The only thing clear was the force of her desire, a boiling power that made her feel vibrant and alive. She emerged with a smile on her lips and peeked at the mirror. She struck a couple of manly poses and found how easy it was to pass for a boy. But now she couldn't stop wondering why such a complete transformation had taken place in her.

She looked herself in the eyes searching for some trace that would still allow her to recognize herself, to know who she was, or had she ceased to be Antonia from having changed sex over night? And how would she confront this new life? How would she go out into the streets of Mexico City, deal with her friends, her bosses, her ex-boyfriends, her landlady, the beggar on the corner? How lucky she was that her two brothers lived abroad, that she had almost no family. But how would she explain to everyone else the only explanation that occurred to her: that she had once wished to become a man—well, she objected, as well an astronaut, a bacteriologist, a movie star—and in some unknown way this wish had turned out to be so powerful that it became real and at the same time so secret that she was unaware of growing up with it?

She was still concentrating on her own eyes, on the tunnel of their dark pupils, as if they were the only passage that could transport her to other times of a mindless and steamrolling certainty. But it didn't last long: the tunnel was now widening and the pupils appeared opening into new zones of undefined shadow. She didn't know why, but the possibility of the unknown excited her to the point of feeling that she was about to take a great leap. To open her arms wide to take in the horizon and make it her own. A bolt of lightning arose between her legs. She almost lost her breath from the new urgency of her hard-on, that overwhelming will to quench a thirst that was until then unknown.

3

She looked through her closet for the most impersonal clothes she owned. Jeans, a plain white blouse, a dark boxy jacket with plain buttons, a pair of loafers she only wore when not going to work, soothed her anxiety. She chose the baggiest panties she had, but even though the bulge between her legs had returned to a state of repose, it still got in her way. She decided to wear nothing under her pants. She'd have to buy some briefs at the store. She put her shoulder-length hair into a ponytail, an acceptable style then for those men who felt like letting their hair grow long. She looked through her purse and took out her car keys and billfold. She put the keys back, for she wanted to confront the city and its people with her own steps. Would she be able to use her credit cards and driver's license? Having never worn much make-up, the face shown on the photos of those plastic cards seemed more childlike than her own, as if only the passing of time marked the difference between the moment when the picture had been taken and the present. But there was also the name, that "Antonia Velarde Rojas," next to the initial that indicated her supposed sex: "F." "F" for female, or "F" for freak? She shuffled the plastic cards between her fingers. If life could get so complicated over just an ounce of flesh, perhaps it was worth the trouble to remain ambiguous. Who would dare touch her between the legs to test her real condition? "Nobody," Antonia told herself, "unless, of course, I want them to."

In the mean time, the street and the world awaited. Just as she was going out she stopped: while deciding what direction her life would take, it might be better to call in sick to work. She hesitated a moment: there were some savings for a trip she'd been planning to take abroad, she could also sell her car, but still there weighed one of those previous worries that had always made her mull over every possibility. Her voice was deeper and more serious, enough for the secretary to swallow the story that she'd come down with a terrible case of laryngitis. The undeniable fact of this new change made her wince. Finally there was also the option of acting like a man. But how could one learn to do that when not so born? Antonia felt lost in the living room of her apartment. Whom could she call for help? Her parents had died in a car accident a couple years earlier, her two brothers—with whom she'd had almost no contact since the painful event—well, one lived in London and the other in Oregon, and she didn't know anybody she could trust with such a delicate matter. She recalled that while attending the university she'd once read a novel, a kind of chivalric romance, and that copy of *Amadis de Gaul* must have been around somewhere. Perhaps in it she could find a role model (of course with neither sword nor armor...at least obvious ones). She searched her bookshelves until she found the book. After leafing through it she put it back in place, thinking, "Well, instead of me being rescued, I have to be the rescuer. Can men really believe they have the duty to save another person?" She bit the thought—if not to say her tongue—for she quickly recognized that although she enjoyed a certain autonomy, all her love relations had failed because in some way she had always hoped to be saved, chosen, rescued, seen, appreciated, discovered, in an immeasurable, irrational use of the passive voice. And so what, now she had to be the active subject, the dominant nucleus of the amorous statement, the powerful knight who charges forward? She laughed to think of Mario, a colleague at work who although not gay seemed like a delicate flower trembling in the wind. She looked suspiciously at the spine of the book. So? She had to start somewhere. She discerned through the window a clear sky and took an umbrella from the coat rack. And with no concern about being thought crazy (Antonia wondered whether she would be a "madman" or a "madwoman"; was the change as simple as that?), she tried to hold it like a lance ready for attack. It wasn't in Amadis, but she remembered reading or hearing somewhere else about an uncommon knight, with shining armor and a white crest upon his helmet, able to vanquish every rival. She couldn't think of his name, but did recall that when stripped of armor, the knight turned out to be an Amazon.* "Well, she might even have been named Antonia," she told herself, laughing as she went down the steps.

---

*The reader needn't suffer for Antonia's bad memory. The character is called Bradamante and one can read about some of her unique adventures in Italo Calvino's *Orlando Furioso*.

4

Where did that ease come from, that lightness not to take things tragically, that brave security that made her feel that she was entitled to a place in the world? (She'd just run into one of her neighbors to whom, after a brief hello, she kept going, undisturbed about the strange look he aimed at her.) Was it because she now inhabited the body of a man or because of the possibility of change, of a metamorphosis that would allow her to be reborn and give her permission to become someone else? (Now she had stopped at the corner newsstand, where the owner's daughter smiled at her with a mixture of curiosity and surprise.) Or was it perhaps the madness of perceiving that logic had modified its coordinates and that in this slippery terrain of possibility it was better to slide by than resist? And she literally skated: she was passing in front of a restaurant when a woman washing the sidewalk carelessly tossed a bucket of water. Antonia jumped, but coming down she slipped in all the suds running toward the sewer. The umbrella flew through the air while she fell to the ground upon her brand new body.

"Sorry, young man. Are you all right?" said the woman, running up to help. As she bent over her breasts bumped into Antonia. "How did it ever occur to you to walk right in front of me? Didn't you see me washing here?"

Antonia watched her squeeze the moisture from his jacket and then, leaning forward, do the same to his pants.

"Where does it hurt? Here?" said the woman while she rubbed the side of his wet leg, sliding her hand up towards his ass. An old lady walking by with a shopping bag looked at them sternly. Antonia grabbed her hands and said thanks. The woman smiled sympathetically and hurried to pick up the umbrella that had landed a few steps away.

"I'm so sorry. Let me offer you something to drink before the manager arrives."

Antonia took the umbrella and returned the smile before adding, "No big deal. Maybe another day."

"As you say—another day."

Antonia started on her way. Just as she was moving away from the restaurant came the sound of another bucket of water coming from behind, but this time the water ran to her feet in a swell as soft as a sigh. Intrigued, she turned toward the woman. "My name is Enedina," she heard. Still a bit confused, Antonia could only smile. So was it that easy for men?

5

Prancing, besieging, courtship, gallantry…Of course she had experienced them as a woman, but always as a state of siege, a conquest where resistance, a stretch-relax-tense-release, established the dynamic of a veiled dance. The tango came to mind, that dance so singularly allusive to copulation, where the woman can only let herself be carried off, follow the lead, the command for a spin or a step masked by a small pressure to the waist or back. Nothing to do with the episode she'd just lived through with the woman at the restaurant where the provocative invitation, the belligerent offering, added an unexpected note.

Besides, just in case there remained any doubt, she had been identified as a man. An act as simple and certain as if she'd been tapped on the shoulder and made a knight. She stopped in front of a pharmacy window. Before, when she was a woman, it took effort to manage the sensuality and desire she stirred in men. Now she curiously contemplated the reflection of the long silhouette in the window between the medicine bottles and flasks of perfume. She found herself attractive as a man—at least as a woman she would have liked the image of himself—and, almost instinctively, tried to frown and adjust the neck on her blouse. She felt at ease, and lifting a hand to pluck a hair from her shoulder noticed out of the corner of her eye some other man imitating him. She stuck out her chest in a gesture of instantaneous attack, but looking more closely tripped upon her own image projected in a mirror off to the side. She smiled at the reflection, thinking, "What the hell, so I have to be careful of my own acting like a tough guy."

A few blocks further on she came across a subway entrance and decided to go down. Like in so many stations in Mexico City's subterranean network, peddlers displayed on the floor of the corridor a variety of merchandise: stationery, candy, eyeglasses, hand-held fans, t-shirts printed with logos and sayings, cassettes and CDs of every sort of music, as well as a bookstall where she went to browse. As she reached for a book, a man came over to ask if she needed any help. Their gazes crossed. The swarthy guy with lank hair murmured, "Antonia, is that you?"

She jumped back instinctively, arching her eyebrows as she tried to recognize him.

"Francisco?" she asked a bit hesitatingly. It had been years since they'd last seen each other during those worry-free times at the university and to run into him precisely the first day of her transformation was hard to believe. No, besides this man was gray-haired and quite fat. Wasn't it rather one of his older brothers?

The man nodded and stayed there expectantly. Antonia remembered how well they'd always gotten along, so much so that during their first couple years of studies they used to hang out together all the time, making their respective partners jealous as well as the rest of their friends who incredulously looked at such trust and intimacy suspicious. Antonia felt that more than a stroke of luck, this was a sign.

"How did you recognize me?" she dared ask.

"Well, you've changed a bit…"

"It's not what you're thinking…"

"I'm not sure what I think…but this new meeting deserves a beer and a chat, no?"

"Do you have time now?" asked Antonia a bit cheered up.

Instead of answering, Francisco went over to a stationery stand and after exchanging a few words with the boy working there came back.

"All set. Let's go, but first tell me something."

Antonia frowned defensively: had they perhaps each changed so much that it might get in the way of reconnecting, calling for the need of extensive explanations, for the cuirass made necessary by caution and distrust? Looking at her from head to toe, Francisco spit out with a complicit look that Antonia knew well, "Why the hell are you carrying an umbrella on such a sunny day? Or is it a lance to slay dragons now that you've been…knighted?"

They went to a bar. It was just past noon, but already several regulars were settled in at the tables drinking and playing dominoes. In its own way the place was kind of cozy: a smooth soothing pool of light where each object and person occupied its own place. They sat down at a table apart from the others and ordered a couple of beers.

"When's the last time we saw each other?" Francisco asked to pick up the conversation.

"I don't know…at the university?"

"No, we saw each other after that. A couple of times at Marcela's, before she married Juan Medrano and fell off the face of the earth. And then we met at the gallery where your boyfriend was having a show. What was his name? Eduardo?"

Antonia nodded. The waiter brought their beers along with a bowl of peanuts. She noticed his moustache was neatly trimmed and thought of all the time that man must have stood before the mirror holding a razor and scissors. She couldn't help but rub a finger above her lip. Indeed the trace of an incipient moustache was growing beneath her nose. She looked at Francisco, who was rather lightly whiskered.

"Do you still see Ricardo Luna? Weren't you two good friends?" she asked, grabbing a handful of peanuts and tossing them into her mouth.

"Ricardo? That's a long story. Or rather a short one. He decided to break off with everyone after coming out of the closet and…" Francisco abruptly paused. "Excuse me, I didn't mean to say… Let's instead toast to meeting again. Cheers…"

They clinked bottles. After taking a sip, Francisco got up the courage to look at Antonia carefully. She noticed and quickly took another swig straight from the bottle. She'd done so secretly when she was a girl, but now as an adult she was used to leaving aside the glass that the waiters automatically brought. She felt the bottle's cool lips on her own and that seemed a more agreeable contact than the glass's airy, distant kiss.

"And so?" she asked, putting her beer down. "What's the verdict?"

"Antonia, I'm not accusing anyone. Weren't we friends? Don't you know me?"

"Yeah, all right…but anyways, go on."

Francisco took a deep breath before continuing, "Fine. What happened to you? Did you take hormones?"

Antonia let out a cheerful burst of laughter. "Hormones? No...
And I didn't have an operation or anything like that. It's really kind
of unbelievable..."

6

Sándor Marai writes that everything between a man and a woman
takes place under conditions similar to haggling in the market, while
the deep feeling of friendship between men is precisely altruism, a
kind of wordless alliance. Whether because the characterizations
of the sexes begin with such broad generalizations that anything
can be put up their vast sleeves, or because the nature of the feelings that Francisco had professed toward Antonia in the past had to
do with authentic friendship, the fact is that he chose to withhold
judgment and only concern himself with the fate that awaited his
old friend.

After a couple more beers, Antonia got up to go to the bathroom. Out of habit she went to the women's room, but before pushing open the door she stopped. There were the symbols for ladies/
gentlemen, like the unavoidable doors of destiny, but in the present
situation which to choose? Seeing the hesitation, Francisco quickly
came over. He tapped her on the shoulder to follow him. A line of
urinals confronted Antonia with their enigmatic faces.

So now she'd have to urinate into those objects possessing such
a disturbing identity? Because if indeed as a woman Antonia had
seldom come across urinals, what's certain is they had always provoked opposing reactions in her: at once unavoidable attraction and
violent repulsion: the secret world of men seen from the perspective
of the disposable and prohibited. As well there were the undeniably
voluptuous shapes of the urinals: did men notice that? Were they

seduced by the sinuous lines or did they only relieve themselves in some mechanical act that negated the object's inherent eroticism? Francisco decided to take a pee, but discretely unzipped. Antonia got ready to imitate him a couple urinals down, but whether it was because she'd never urinated in one or because she wasn't confident enough to go in front of Francisco, the fact is her penis refused to empty her bladder.

"Don't worry. That happens to everyone when there's some guy right beside us and we think he's looking," said Francisco while he shook his member and then put it back in his pants before zipping up with the skill of a magician.

Antonia had to concentrate. To urinate in front of someone else is almost always an arduous task, but when one has changed bodies there's nothing left to do but try, but continue risking the leaden feet of logic and shoe them with the volatile skin of chance. She shut her eyes and breathed so deeply that she felt the air reaching the bottom of her guts and with it an expansive sensation of well-being. Then she started to go. She opened her eyes to confirm the miracle: the stream was coming out forcefully and hitting the sides of that porcelain shell especially prepared to receive it. Her hand directed the stream as if she were painting the urinal coat by coat. She exhaled with pleasure at this new discovery: more than just satisfying a need, the act confirmed in her a will capable of incurring or overturning, of taking possession of that new majestic territory of curving lines that so evoked—she admitted to herself a bit confused—the hips of a woman. She felt like she'd crossed over an unknown boundary. She looked at her member with fascination: what other surprises did it hide?

"So you're learning already…It's a great friend, but not always a faithful one," Francisco murmured from behind.

7

How is the disguise of a man constructed? Antonia wished that she had an instruction manual. It would have made her life easier, as she imagined happened with the rituals of bullfighting or chivalry. Bullfighting had never attracted her; on the other hand knights, ah, the damsel's desirous calling to be saved by one, made her imagine the process of inverting the roles and, to begin with, dressing accordingly. She mentally went through the terms—falconry, the arts of meat carving and poetry, all of which seemed medieval and ancient, and lacking an "art of chivalry," or more properly an "art of dressing and shoeing knights," she thought of visiting a museum.

Standing before the display cases she discovered various kinds of armor, from simple chain mail cloaks that fell to the knee to complete body armor that included gloves and metal shoes. In many cases, according to the information placards, the armor presented two aspects: the protection of the person wearing it and the exhibition of his wealth. The refinement of a helmet, the master work of a sword, completed the all-powerful and invulnerable image. But if a knight wearing armor fell to the ground, it was hard to get up by himself.

Antonia then chose a lighter Gothic suit of armor and stood before the display case in such a way that her reflection coincided with the piece on exhibit. It was a midweek day, so the scant visitors allowed her to try finding the right distance several times. When she finally did and the coat sat perfectly upon her, it occurred to her to make a gesture as if taking her sword from its sheath. Ah… what a proud and beautiful act to reveal, displaying one's sword in all its splendor. She stayed there in a daze for a few moments. Then she began to walk along in her imaginary armor, carrying it at first with dignity and careful attention until little by little, due to its weight and rigidity, which almost dislocated one of her hips, she finally had to set it down with weariness and spite. While she took off the bulky garments, or rather while she tried to strip off the cuirass, the helmet she still wore on her head fell to the floor and rolled along loudly like a metallic burst of laughter. At least that's what it seemed like to Antonia, who feeling disconcerted continued watching the moving helmet until it stopped at the feet of a woman, a museum guard who happened to find herself peering around the entrance to the gallery of armor and had been watching him the whole time practicing his imaginary knightly ritual. Antonia had to put on a brave face while leaving the hall before the woman's smiling gaze.

"Young man…you forgot your sword," said the guard, suddenly serious, pointing a finger at an object that Antonia had brought and leaned against a display case.

Antonia remembered then her umbrella and went back for it. She mumbled a timid "thanks" and left the museum as quickly as possible.

On the way home, a bit disturbed by that sudden fascination with suits of armor, she wondered if that's what she really wanted, just to put on the disguise of a man. The armor was beautiful: one could wear it, at least in imagination, at certain moments of attack from the outside, but beyond that, wasn't it a stereotype of masculinity? And was that really what interested her: to cover up again, to feign? To learn on what side men button their shirts? What foot they get out of bed with? How many sheep they count before falling asleep? On the other hand, if now indeed she was inhabiting the body of a man, with the metamorphosis had she entered an acute phase of amnesia, forgetting all her past and ceasing to be the person she'd been? Antonia suddenly realized there was no change without memory. In fact, life had placed before her an alternative to madness and she could believe herself as unreal as a character in a fantasy novel or accept that the rules of the game had simply changed and thus confront the consequences. She would no longer menstruate, undoubtedly she had a penis, but she also recognized within herself an irrepressible desire to venture forth and explore. (Was this a compensation of the spirit in knight errantry?) She could imagine that the boundless desire to know the desire of the other had woven the strings holding up this new appearance, or that the mines excavated so deeply by envy had finally struck an alchemical wealth…But what was certain, or rather what was uncertain, was the thing attracting her, the dull roar that precedes the wave rising to our shoulders…And then? To see how far she was going to be carried away, to know what she was capable of and then—perhaps—discover in the turbulent waters the substance of her most profound desires.

A Urinal This Side of Duchamp's

1

The first urinal Antonia recalled seeing wasn't the actual object but a photograph of that of Marcel Duchamp's during a slide show in a course called Aesthetic Currents. Of course, being a woman it wasn't easy to come across them in public bathrooms. Among the carrousel of images that shone on the screen that morning in class, Antonia felt touched by the blind, dazzling gaze of the porcelain face that she didn't recognize.

A ritualistic mask? The stylized sculpture of an animal head or a piece of fruit? She asked herself these questions when she felt less stunned. But the carrousel kept going around and the words of her professor had little to do with that scrutinized mystery, except for the innovation of a French avant-garde artist who took objects from daily reality and unveiled their previously hidden beauty, throwing into question the conventional notion of the artistic.

Her second encounter took place just a couple of days later at a café on Plaza Washington. There, amidst the noise of some friends from the university she'd met to go over a report on some readings, she glimpsed through a door left open a bit ajar by the last user a unique space: a white tile bathroom from which emerged a receptacle similar to Duchamp's work, except upside down. She stood and went towards it hypnotized. Not understanding why, she locked the door behind herself and remained powerless before that object gaping there, absorbed in its own vanity.

She found a handle and tried to make it work. Water flowed quietly around the contours according to a mechanism of gravity and fluidity that Antonia found erotic: the abandonment to the force of a will not our own, the loss of one's self in the dark hole of the most absolute dissolution. Then, as she looked into the drain, she smelled the intense odor emanating from the inner walls: a wave sour and corrosive, but also sweet, that took her breath away. In face of the shining immanence and repulsion it provoked, Antonia recalled several names: urinary, urinal, fount…She suddenly knew that those verbal realities corresponded to this concave face, deep and hidden, that in the end was also looking at her.

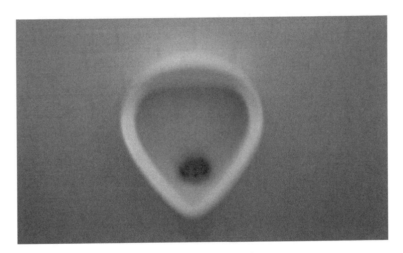

2

So many greetings and conversations with the urinals awaited her now in the men's rooms. And in each one the feeling of power when pouring out, a release that made her believe the world was ready for and conditioned to her needs.

She came across urinals of many types and shapes, from the stainless steel communal trough to individual founts that weren't attached to the wall but rather emerged like magnolia buds from the floor, whose sensual forms stirred the temptation to commit delectable, illicit acts.

There were also those that extended vertically all the way to the floor and other ultra-modern ones activated simply by stopping to urinate in them. But although the forms varied, Antonia perceived the purity of line, the concentrated, continuous voluptuousness passively ready to receive, their nature always to be ready.

Despite the neatness of some bathrooms, the persistent smell of concentrated urine emanated like the reminder that beauty always has its morbid side. (And on the contrary, that everything repulsive we're hit by exudes its own beauty.)

In bars she frequently ran into a humorous variation: ice cubes that presumably saved water piled up inside the urinals that one could aim at with the stream of urine as if shooting at a target, or a whole block of ice whose transparent form one could penetrate for the simple pleasure of boring a hole, or playing the sculptor melt the rough edges and mould forms according to the heat and duration of the stream. She learned from Carlos Díaz, an airplane pilot she'd met thanks to Francisco, that in Holland some urinals had the etching of a fly so one could aim at the target inside. He also told her about those enclosed in glass on the top floor of the Seattle Tower, where one could pee with the mischievous sensation of letting it go over the city that sprawled to the horizon. In contrast to such eccentricities, she learned about El Incendio, a practical cantina in Guanajuato whose urinal was an open pipe at the foot of the bar, so that after a couple beers the patrons had only to say "excuse me" and lower their zipper and not worry about splashing.

In any the case, Antonia couldn't face a urinal without the encounter troubling her, for its condition as an object of exclusively masculine use reminded her of that liminal space, that boundary where new desires and appetites made her splash the water before deciding whether to jump right in or go no further. Unclear exactly where her interests in urinals might lead, she took advantage of any and all opportunity to familiarize herself with them. Like the time Francisco introduced her to Carlos Díaz and Raimundo Ventura, two friends the bookseller deemed necessary for Antonia's apprenticeship in this new phase of life.

"Carlos is a pilot. He's well-traveled and a great guy. Raimundo, too, he's a pretty crazy photographer but a good artist," Francisco told her, pushing the revolving door of the bar where they were supposed to meet. "I've given it some thought and these two can help you."

"Help me? Do they know a lot about urinals? How strange, because from what I've seen they don't stir much interest in men."

"Tell me what you prefer. We say you used to be a woman and now…"

"No. Let's just see what happens."

3

"Urinals? So what do you want to know? They're like women—you use them and that's that," responded Carlos before letting

22

out a laugh, but then he added, "Careful. I didn't say that. It was Matatías, the macho that every proud man carries within himself and who comes out of me from time to time."

Antonia observed him in fascination. He had the virtue of saying any series of horrible things and still be charming.

"And what other characters do you carry inside?" Antonia dared to ask while they were served the first round of drinks.

"Aha. What a clever boy. What did you say your name was?" parried Carlos with a natural thrust.

Antonia became nervous again, just as when Francisco had introduced her. Although she hadn't given the matter much thought, her real name unconsciously began to slip out, but she stopped midword before finishing: "Anton…" She started to say it doubtfully, but then finished emphatically, "Antón…"

"Antón? You from a Russian family?" asked Raimundo, who until then had only been observing Antonia with interest.

"No…Let's say it was a whim of my mother," she replied, exchanging a complicit glance with Francisco. "She used to read novels by Dostoevski and short stories by Chekov."

"Sure, sure. So you were nursed on Slavic literature. That's not a bad start."

"Well, a toast to our meeting," said Carlos, raising his bottle and clinking it with the others'.

As soon as Antonia took a drink, she again went on the charge. "But Carlos, you haven't answered my question—what other characters do you have within you?"

Carlos flashed a smile revealing teeth so white and straight that Antonia thought that they were gleaming at her.

"A lot," he said, pausing in an unusual display of shyness. "You'll get to know them one at a time. For now, just be happy to meet Carlos the Combatant, because from what I've learned from Francisco, you need an instructor for your arts of chivalry. And for all that, why are you so interested in urinals? Remember Matatías—that's not something for well-behaved men."

Antonia exhaled loudly. "To make a long story short, before I turned twelve I was a real dwarf, and so had a long time to observe and grow fond of them from the impossible vantage point of such an unequal relation," she recollected. "No, the truth is they fascinate me."

Raimundo couldn't help but laugh. "So that's how it is," he said, directing a warm look of recognition at Antonia. "I hadn't though about it. A series of photos of urinals would be interesting. An homage to Duchamp and Stieglitz, but also something more. The bottom line is they exude their own sensuality."

Antonia turned towards him surprised. Raimundo had fleshy lips and a gaze that poked around into more than just the surface of things. Francisco smiled, pleased, as if he'd imagined the scene beforehand: he hadn't been wrong to think those two men would get along well with Antonia.

"Carlos, as a pilot you've been to so many different places that you must have seen lots of urinals. Are they alike around the world?" asked Francisco.

"Of course I recall urinals from the places I've flown to." The eyes of Carlos flitted from one person to another and an exultant happiness breathily promised a treasure of accumulated stories and adventures. "In restaurants, bars, hotels, highway rest stops, pool halls, bowling alleys, gas stations, train stations...I remember especially two in Madrid. Right behind the Chicote is the bar Diego's, which makes a great drink and where there are some ultramodern urinals, so fresh-smelling and clean you could drink the water from them. These marvelous machines are made of stainless steel and automatically flush as soon as you start pissing. With more respect than affection I also recall the bathrooms in Retiro Park: a pretty house, like a flower in the middle of a garden where there was the sweatiest, sourest stench of urine I've ever smelled. Like a porcupine fart, an odor of old beer and death roll down the shuttered windows. And if you dare enter, Antón, you'll see something like the vapor of dry ice, a junkie smoking crack or beating off, and several badly aged classic urinals that look like little guillotines. Sometimes it's too scary there to take a piss."

Antonia looked at him in rapture. If she were still a woman she'd fall in love with this man who could so resurrect such an encounter with memory. Besides, he was quite handsome. In spite of his forty-odd years, he had a vigorous body and a welcoming smile that invited intimacy. After a few seconds she turned her attention to Raimundo, who winked at her with a shared admiration.

"So then," said Raimundo while he took out a camera that Antonia hadn't noticed. "But now confess to Antón who really said that, because isn't it true, Francisco, it wasn't really Carlos that just impressed us with such verbal boasting?"

"No...maybe Julio, or who's the writer you're into now?" replied Francisco, playing along with Raimundo.

"No way, fuck off. You think you know me but you don't...neither Julio nor Augustus. Today it was me my very self," and he hesitated a moment. "What did I tell you I was called yesterday? Ah, yes, Don Carlos Díaz de Vivar. To your health." And he raised his bottle as the others laughing joined him in toast.

As soon as they finished their beers, Raimundo signaled to the waiter for another round.

"Listen, Antón, if you're so interested in urinals maybe you should take some photos yourself. There's no better way of knowing things than photography. You think you're taking the picture, but it's really the eye of the camera that perceives and captures. In good photos disturbing things are found, like in dreams."

"You mean go shoot the urinals here?" asked Antonia enthusiastically.

"If you want, I'll lend you my camera," he said, holding it out. "And maybe we could arrange some tours. What do you think, you guys want to join us?"

Francisco argued that he couldn't just drop things at work. And when their gazes fell on Carlos, the pilot exclaimed almost reactively, "Go photograph urinals? You're crazy—what are you, fags or perverts? If I'm going to take an interest in something, I find bidets more curious—such strange porcelain objects where women wash their private parts before or after making love. To think of a woman straddling a bidet—now that I find tremendously erotic."

"Fine," Raimundo broke in condescendingly, "but there aren't many bidets in Mexico City. And besides, except for Brassäi,* very few people have paid attention to that peculiar shape with such an obvious erotic charge. And yes, it'd also be worth doing a series of photos on that subject, but I'm quite afraid we'd have to inquire about them in the few Porfirian houses that still have bathrooms

---

*Raimundo is referring to the Hungarian photographer Gyula Halasz, known as Brassäi (1899-1984), and in particular his recollection of the image entitled "La toilette dans un hôtel de passe. Rue Quincampoix." Paris, c. 1932.

from the era. Or, clearly, travel to Paris, Rome…you can still find bidets used there. On the other hand, you find urinals everywhere. You just said so yourself."

Antonia kept silent. She furrowed her brow and holding the camera she rather looked like a little boy with a ball who's just been told he can't go out and play with his friends. Carlos gazed at her a few moments and then relented. "All right, all right. There are some rather unique urinals in the Palace of Fine Arts. If you're searching for something suggestive, you should start there…"

4

Lying in bed, Antonia reflected that what had happened to her was like moving into a new house. To find a new place for personal things, accustom one's steps to the texture of the hallway, discover what corner of the living room is most comfortable. And on a night like that, after all the bustle of arranging the furniture, to look at the ceiling in the dark like a distant vault in which we have yet to find our place. But did she ever have that? Perhaps not, but the certitude that she used to possess kept her from such questioning and let her act in that doubtless animal dimension: a cat lying in the sunshine, unconcerned about the threat of rain.

Instead her existence now resembled a sort of labyrinth, the entering of unknown territory with no possibility of discerning a goal or exit. She recalled the myth of Theseus, who had entered the labyrinth of Crete in order to kill the Minotaur. Besides his gleaming sword, Theseus carried the thread of Ariadne, the princess whose love for him increased the closer she imagined him to death. Armed in valor, Theseus walked through the narrow passages, confronted the Minotaur, killed it and then picked up the thread in order to find his way out. But when he turned back, Theseus had already become someone else. What had he discovered during that passage? Could he feel no pity when he slit the throat of the beast with a human gaze? Did he recognize in that face his own concealed animality? Antonia gestured restlessly: she put her hand on her testicles and began scratching them. It was delightful, although her crotch didn't itch. Standing before the entrance to the labyrinth, there was nothing to do but enter and take a risk. Expose herself to the fact that she was the Minotaur in those unknown parts and that instead of burying her in obscurity, the darkness illuminated her.

5

To give herself some courage, she resolved to take the umbrella with her to the office. She concocted some health reasons for her boss, who contemplating her so changed accepted her quitting as some shameful event better not talked about. They allowed her to collect her personal items. As she headed to the elevator, one of the secretaries on the floor caught up to her.

"I don't know what you did, but it looks good," she flirted once the automatic doors closed.

Antonia was completely lost in herself but still found her gaze drawn to the woman's plunging neckline and her ample bosom pressed together. It was as if those breasts spoke to her in a tumultuous murmur, as if they woke her sleeping feelings, lulling them with an overwhelming promise.

It was to them and not the woman that she responded with a "thanks" and an involuntary erection that she hid with the box holding her possessions. The woman got off two floors down and Antonia could finally catch her breath.

She left the building. The umbrella hung from her arm and the box was still hiding her swollen penis when Francisco pulled up in his car to get her.

"Sure you know what you're doing?" he asked while trying to help her put everything on the back seat.

"I don't know…I don't know if I'll ever be sure of anything again." Antonia's voice sounded deeper than usual. She wanted to cry but couldn't imagine breaking down in front of her friend. Before, when she was a woman, it wasn't easy either to ask for help, to recognize the need for affection and companionship. Francisco read her thoughts.

"One favor, Antón." It was the first time he'd used that name. "Don't cry. Everyone supposes the world has changed and now we men are entitled to our emotions. But crying is for queers."

Antonia felt like her muscles were hardening, as if a suit of armor had immobilized her to the point where she could only breathe enough not to choke. Francisco drove on in silence until they got to a subway station, where he got out of the car.

"Here's the address of the book warehouse in La Lagunilla," he said, handing her a folded piece of paper. "I'm glad you can help me with this part of the business. It doesn't pay much but it lets me live well and even save a little. I told them you'd come by around noon, so you have time to go get Raimundo at his studio. He told me he wants to tour downtown with you."

Antonia took the paper and sat before the steering wheel. She waited for Francisco to disappear down the stairs before casting a glance at the backseat. Photos, books and papers spilled from the box in a mess, because that's how she'd flung them right after removing them from the office. She felt like throwing it all in the first garbage can she came across. Perhaps she should do the same with the umbrella. All things considered, it hadn't proved very useful. She tried to reach it, but the metallic arm of the armor kept her from moving very easily. She felt stiff and uncomfortable, but at least she was protected.

6

They wandered around the antiques market at La Lagunilla before visiting the warehouse of used books. A timid magic, disguised in dust and ruin, that exultant, silent life of used objects, sprawled before them in the form of furniture, glassware, cameras, paintings, horseshoes, armoires, jewelry, ex-votos, deeds from the epoch of Porfirio Díaz. On the far side of the stalls Antonia noticed a shop selling masks and suggested to the photographer going there. They had just stepped inside when they came across a wall covered in wooden faces indolently sleeping before the drudgery of life. Many of them represented the humanized hybrids of animals and heavenly bodies that allowed one to glimpse metamorphosis as an anxiety of fusion and power. Clearly dazzled, Raimundo indicated to Antonia a dark mask that emulated the full belly of a pregnant woman. The openings for the eyes were placed in the breast area. The closer he got to it, the more intrigued he became and was just about to ask the owner to take it down for him.

"It's from Africa," the man remarked with a haughty expression, and then he said to a girl cleaning with a colorful feather duster some little porcelain masks in a display case off to one side, "Leave that be and take it down."

Seen from behind, the girl was a teen-ager so thin that her bone structure glimmered beneath her supple, radiant skin. Despite the absence of curves, perhaps hidden by the overalls she was wearing, the girl possessed a decided femininity that obliged Raimundo and Antonia to let her by when she turned around and confronted them with her smiling body. Her hair was short but grown out in a fringe that hung to one side in a gesture of subtle flirtatiousness. She'd just started to pick up a folding ladder resting beside the entrance to the backroom when Raimundo offered to help. The girl assented and let him put it at the foot of the masks; then she climbed it with a playful ease and asked which mask to bring down. Raimundo hurried to point it out without taking his eyes from her. She took the mask in her hands and did something unexpected—she brought it to her face and held it there for several seconds.

"It feels good to be pregnant," she said from behind the dark, gravid belly.

"It fits you well," replied Raimundo with a smile, fumbling for his camera while asking, "May I?"

From the backroom they heard the owner's voice saying, "Cornelius, come here."

The mask turned its unusual and disquieting pregnancy toward the man. Having watched the scene in fascination, Antonia hurried to extend a hand.

"Can I help you down?" she asked while Raimundo hung the camera strap back over his shoulder.

"Of course I knew right away it was a boy, not you?" murmured Raimundo while he picked up a book with a leather cover. They'd stopped at a used bookstall and the volume he was examining was a study on anatomy printed in Madrid at the end of the nineteenth century.

Antonia was about to admit her mistake but then the armor chafed against her flanks. "Well, at first I was unsure, but then it became obvious."

"Yeah, when you heard that guy call him Cornelius and not Cornelia, no?" Raimundo answered, not paying much attention to her words. In contrast, a look of concentration crossed over his face when he discovered that the book had reproductions of prints by a Renaissance anatomist, Andrea Vesalio.

Antonia didn't notice how absorbed the photographer was and cracked a smile: before, when she was a woman, she took pride in recognizing immediately any circumspect transvestite or gay man that crossed her path. She remembered that she was carrying the plastic bag with the mask Raimundo had bought and she discerned beneath the folds of wrapping paper the swelling stomach that now pulsed obscurely in her hands.

"If you knew he wasn't a woman," she replied, not taking her eyes from the mask, "then why did you carry over the ladder and look at him so much?"

"I like to play around, don't you?" Raimundo replied while his fingers poked through the volume and absently leafed through the pages; suddenly they stopped on a drawing. "Besides, are you going to deny that Cornelius was charming?"

Raimundo turned toward Antonia, and looking her in the eye repeated the word. "Yes, charming. Now leave me alone. Not even my ex-wives gave me as hard a time as you do."

Antonia felt exposed and instinctively tried to tighten the armor: she thrust out her body and clenched her fists, ready to attack, but then Raimundo turned around to immerse himself in the book he had been looking through.

"You're not going to believe it, Antón," he said with a laugh while pointing at something in the anatomical drawing. "What does that remind you of?"

Antonia stiffly approached. There on the page appeared the image of a receptacle that looked quite like a urinal. She couldn't help but feel amazed to recognize that the drawing formed part of an undoubtedly phallic oblong member. But what she read below the figure surprised her even more, for it wasn't a penis as she first thought, but a sectioned uterus. "Transversal section of the womb," she sacramentally recited from the caption beneath the drawing.* Still incredulous, she turned to Raimundo and insisted, "A womb? Haven't they mixed up the images?"

But can whoever thinks about it a moment have any doubt? As Antonia would discover later, in the 1914 notes for his "Green Box," Duchamp had written, "One only has: for female the public urinal and one lives by it." It's worth saying once and for all: the urinal, which has a purely masculine usage, possesses a gender and it's feminine.

It occurred to Raimundo, thinking he'd made some luminous discovery that morning in La Lagunilla, that it might be worthwhile to bring an archeologist along to the urinals in order to learn how long they had been in existence, what had been the first designs, which materials were used in their construction and, above all, to imagine exactly how much the creator of the most common models had in mind a feminine stamp—perhaps this very drawing by Vesalio—for the shape of that receptacle, womb, shell, where men discharged and spilled themselves in an automatic, almost loving, act of pleasure.

7

Despite exploring and photographing a considerable gamut of urinals, Antonia preferred those which retained their original form of a womb, of caressingly full, firm hips, made disturbing by the lubricious porcelain that conferred upon them an organic dampness, the gaping little beasts rendered sensually hypnotic.

Even though the most modern ones exercised a chilling seduction (a few with drains that recalled the folds of a clitoris, vigilant optical scanners, mechanical steps that flushed with the weight of the user), those that most impressed her had a clear feminine appearance where men spilled their golden rain in an unconscious ritual of release that emulated copulation in the most immediate and animal sense: the consummation of a blind and vehement need, the satisfaction of a pure and urgent desire. It wasn't strange that men didn't give much though to the beauty of those objects and were too hurried before the magic inherent in their ritual. What a pity each time they went to one and discovered that one-eyed, single-throated gaze awaiting them, always ready to receive them, because then they would have to understand that their animality, that nature which they wished to dominate and hold in their fist, existed not only in bed or in their testicles. But to think like that, with this latent erotic charge proven and found everywhere, to live like that, how frightening, what madness.

Standing over the photos she'd taken during the last week, Antonia was beside herself. How right Raimundo had been to say that thanks to the camera she would discover an unknown side of urinals. As if the diaphragm were a hungry cavity that made evident the very essence of desire. And Antonia discovered herself thirsty, desiring. She thought the time would come when she would have to make love like a man, use her member and penetrate a woman as she had so far put it in urinals. She'd finally feel what men felt when they made love. A delectable dizziness seized her, and her hands urged on the only mast they could grab while she imagined giving it to some woman in the men's room and there, after sitting her down in one of the urinals, spreading her legs and taking her.

Lessons in Falconry and the Art of Meat Carving

1

We know much more than we think we know, but often, from childhood on, we forget and are taught to forget everything that in truth bothers us. At least that's what happens with genitalia and desire. When was the first time Antonia saw a penis? The questions surged forth now that she was walking naked to the bathroom, getting ready to lay out the kit on the little washstand to shave the old-fashioned way, following the instructions of Francisco, who'd taken pity after seeing that face ravaged by little cuts: a shaving cup with hot water to wet a facecloth, a brush, scissors, lotions. Antonia threw her head back and placed the hot towel over her jaw. While waiting she acknowledged that she didn't recall a sole face-to-face encounter with the masculine member during childhood or adolescence, but that during her first intimate relation as a woman she'd behaved naturally with it, as if already accustomed to its imminence from other frequent encounters. But to see it or feel it inside was different than possessing one, that pricking, autonomous, surprising, willful extension. How could one not admire its inconstancy that could lead to an urgent pleasure in which she—Antonia—and he—the phallus—melded into a single bolt of lightning? Only then were they truly one. (In contrast, as a woman, pleasure—whether provoked by her or her lovers—was like falling inwards towards an abyss, a sea of concentric waves that carried her towards the dissolution of the being that she herself had always been, one with her body and vagina.)

Now, ordinarily, she perceived her member as a separate being and every morning she contemplated it in the mirror, spreading a bit her legs and pressing together the cheeks of her ass, to affirm its presence and power. Being something exterior, she could show it off and take pride in it, but it also made her feel vulnerable (like that moment when she'd undraped her towel in a rather brusque movement and knocked a pair of scissors into a sinister flight towards her stomach, making her instinctively jump back). "The woman's vagina," she thought, swallowing hard while deciding whether or not to pick up the scissors, "is hidden and for that reason guarded. In contrast, the man's organ"—and she couldn't help but cast a loving glance at her genitals—"is so dangerously exposed…"

Clip, cut, castrate…they had been transformed into ferocious and unbearably threatening words. For a woman, rape—however brutal—couldn't violate more than her own nature. In contrast, take away a man's virility and he was completely destroyed—and if raped, turned female. A double disadvantage: as much in the emasculation as the rape, the man stopped being himself. Antonia bent over the scissors but dared not touch them. She observed how hypnotic the edge was, how paralyzing, how literally breathtaking. A few moments later, having collected herself, she wondered how men could live with such a risk. We know much more than we think we know, but we forget. She recalled the bragging of her brothers, that unfurling cockiness when they talked about their penises. Now she understood what was behind all that. She'd unconsciously brought her hands to her member, protecting it in a kind of nest. The phone rang a couple times before she decided to let her little chick loose. From the other end of the line came a familiar voice.

"What's happening, man? It's Carlos. Don't you think you've already photographed enough urinals? Now it's time to learn how to hunt…"

2

They made plans to meet at the opening of a show by a sculptor friend of Raimundo's. Not having been to a gallery since her breakup with Eduardo, Antonia was quite punctual, only to remember that except for the organizers and waiters almost nobody ever arrived on time. She shrugged and took advantage of the solitude of the place to look at the work since besides her, only a group of young people was there. The wood sculptures were overwhelming: fragmented bodies forced into impossibly tense positions with barbed wire. The kids were joking around, perhaps to alleviate the stab of pain provoked by those tormented torsos and hips, but one of the two girls in the group stood there, despite her smile, with her arms crossed beneath a white shawl that at times she used as a cape to protect herself. Antonia didn't know whether it was the gesture of her body or because it formed part of her nature, but it seemed the girl radiated a genuine fragility that had to be guarded. She couldn't help but think of an untouched magnolia blossom.

More people started to arrive, some dressed elegantly, others looking rather scruffy, and some more extravagantly attired. Two men with the bodies of modern dancers walked about bare-chested, daubed with pitch and wearing barbed-wire crowns. Antonia thought they must be part of the performance mentioned in the invitation and moved aside when one of them asked to get by. She ended up behind a sculpture, facing the girl in the white shawl who'd split off from her friends. Antonia noticed that she wore bangs that gave her a childish air and that her immense eyes examined the sculptures with an undeniable anguish. Her arms were still crossed upon her chest, and rather than a young woman she looked like a little girl who'd been brought to a forest so she'd become lost. Surely she shivered in face of the dark desire that those bodies—petrified trees—awakened. Where would she sleep peacefully again after recognizing such deviance?, wondered Antonia in a murmur of thought, already imagining the lurking city, the ululating forest eager to tear at her desirable white skin (but didn't the girl let herself come to the edge of her own desire, boiling with a roar through which her blood beat out a message of conflicting instincts?) Two thoughts crossed Antonia's mind: take the sword from its sheath to protect her (if she had a suit of armor to use when necessary, then why wouldn't she have a sword?), and second, imagine her naked underneath the white shawl, with the pointed breasts and smiling white pubis of a little girl.

Antonia's crotch stirred. "Attack," she heard herself say to her penis as if that were the real sword. "But if I used to be a woman," she heard herself reply. Her member kept swelling and, proud of its power, didn't even dignify her with an answer. Anyway, Antonia thought it was thinking, "O.K., you used to be a woman, but do you really think that's so important?" While Antonia hesitated, her organ kept enlarging until it pressed painfully against the band of her underwear. Even so it insisted, "Look at her tremble, so little and alone. Isn't it true she needs someone to protect her?"

In truth the girl was trembling slightly, but perceptibly. Amidst the noise of the multitude around them—the place was getting more and more crowded—she was naked beneath the shawl and her gaze was a roiled pond. Antonia couldn't avoid looking at herself in its waters, when suddenly the young woman looked behind the sculpture. In a second, the helplessness ceased and Little White Riding Hood showed her muzzle.

"And what are you looking at?" the girl spit out fiercely.

As it took Antonia a moment to respond—the armor's defensive stiffness impeded her from thinking—the girl turned and went off, not without first taking a glass of wine offered by a waiter. He also offered Antonia one. She took the drink and downed it to recover from the stab. She had a sword, but the bottom line was she hadn't known how to use it. She was pulling on her leggings to head somewhere else when Carlos tapped her on the shoulder.

"Well, well," he said. "You were around here after all. Something catch your eye?"

"I'd say the sculptures are rather too disturbing. I wonder who'd actually buy them."

"I don't know. Personally I wouldn't want to wake up and find one in my house, but I was asking you about women, if you'd gone on the hunt yet."

Antonia just shook her head. Carlos searched out her eyes through the bars of the helmet, but Antonia just flashed a smile.

"Let's go then. Raimundo is at the entrance. I want you to meet one of his students. I'm sure you'll find her charming."

Antonia let herself be led through the people. There was no need for Carlos to add something about a little girl cloaked in the mantle of an adult. She was sure that he was going to introduce her to the same girl who minutes earlier had left her disarmed before the battle had even begun.

But she was wrong, or almost. Carlos didn't introduce the girl in the white shawl but her friend, the other girl in the group she'd seen upon arriving to the gallery. They were all students at the art school where Raimundo taught. When the latter saw Antonia, he made a place beside him and put an arm around her shoulders.

"Maestro Antón, what a pleasure," said the photographer before proceeding with the introductions: Julián, Moisés, Bernardo. But when he finally got to the girl, Carlos broke in, "And this is Claudia."

Searching past them to locate the other young woman, Antonia finally looked at Claudia, surprised not to have noticed her before: she had a splendid figure and was wearing a red dress, simple and elegant in front, but whose sole adornment could only be appreciated from behind: a slit that extended from the nape of her neck to the bottom of her back. Antonia didn't discover that at first (although she could appreciate the undeniable figure of the woman before her), but a little later the girl managed to cross through the small circle of friends and, with the pretext of removing a smear of lipstick she'd left on the cheek of Carlos, showed off her magnificent torso from behind. Antonia felt her gaze wander over the small of her back, soft but of a firmness that glowed and blunted all will. She stretched out her hand and touched the girl's back. Claudia turned into a panther and trapped the hand. They all remained silent. Self-assured, with a smile that relaxed everyone else, she said, "Where did they keep you locked up? Just because I like you, I won't bust your face."

3

"No, Antón, Casanova's art isn't some bloody hunting," said Carlos while they ate breakfast at his apartment, where Antonia had slept after a party that followed the opening. "Giacomo observes, measures the possibilities, readies the traps, but in the end it's he who lets himself be hunted. I learned two maxims from his memoirs: take advantage of the opportunity and take the prey only as far as she wants to be forced. Now, as in everything, there is a factor of chance, an element of surprise that makes it all the more passionate. It's like piloting a commercial plane. You're provided the route. You receive instructions from the air traffic controller, but in the end the take off, the flight, and the landing are yours alone..."

"But, Carlos," Antonia interrupted, "how can you say that? Didn't you see how my 'bloody hunting,' as you call it, charmed Claudia? In fact, she was all over me the whole night, while I really wanted to hit on the other girl, Malva."

"Well, that's because women are unpredictable. If I had known she liked getting touched on the back in that marvelous décolleté falling to her ass, I might have tried that, too. Not because I'm so interested in her, but just to try. How did you ever dare?"

"It wasn't me," Antonia tried to explain more to herself than to Carlos. She held out her cup for more coffee. "Lately strange things have been happening to me. It's as if my desires are in charge. I think that's what she liked—discovering that her body awakened, how would you say, a magnetic obedience."

"Perhaps. I've seen that in other women: more than their own desire, they're stunned to discover the desire they provoke in others."

"But that happens with men, too," said Antonia, pausing because it seemed the comment excluded her and she hurried to correct herself. "Well, that's what just happened to me with Claudia. It was a play of mirrors: my uncontrollable desire awakened her curiosity, her vanity, and then her own desire. I felt like an observed man then—" Antonia noticed the natural way she attributed herself a new gender and smiled, happy to be able to joke around with herself "—observed, and desired. As if her eyes were a mirror that reflected a nice image of myself. That's never happened to me before, to feel and be conscious of it all at once."

Antonia became silent. She asked herself if having changed sex without losing her previous experiences now allowed her a con-

43

science more open to being both actor and witness. Carlos got up and put a few rolls in a wicker basket sitting in the middle of the table. Antonia then noticed the order and cleanliness of the space around them. She thought that for living alone—how different than the apartment of Raimundo, who also lived by himself—Carlos was an excellent homemaker.

"I've always said so: love is a mutual narcissism," he said, refilling their cups.

"Love? Why are you talking about love? Last night was just desire, attraction."

"Well, I'm not referring to what happened between you and Claudia, but to what could have happened…"

"If Malva hadn't shown up. But maybe that's why Claudia was so insistent. She must have realized I was more attracted to Malva."

"Yeah, the competition among women. They're friends, didn't you know? Maybe they'll break up now."

Antonia looked at Carlos questioningly.

"Aha, that's what happened once when Raimundo chose Malva for a photo shoot. But if you're more interested in her, you were right to provoke her with the other. Of course, it all depends on what you want."

Carlos drank down the rest of his coffee and flashed a mischievous smile.

"What are you laughing about now?" Antonia asked intrigued.

Carlos let out a sigh before adding, "I'm laughing about Francisco, who was so worried about you. For not knowing anything about seduction, you know more than enough about making yourself desirable."

4

As it was Saturday morning, Carlos suggested they go take a steam bath—one of those purification rites many men were accustomed to after an all-nighter. Antonia hesitated to accept the invitation because apart from the urinals, it would be the first time confronting an exclusively masculine intimate environment. Moreover, it was a matter of naked bodies: hers and those of the others she would encounter there, although the truth was that she was curious and still attracted to men. Since Carlos wouldn't take no for an answer, they ended up going to a place near his apartment.

They entered a common area, each of them with a towel wrapped around the waist. Amidst the fog Antonia discerned several men sitting on mosaic benches conversing among themselves, but as soon as they entered the others fell silent. Carlos waved to a couple of men and took a seat nearby. Antonia sat down beside him, legs spread just like the others. She couldn't help feeling uncomfortable. What would those guys think if they knew she had once been a woman? Would they beat her, insult her, yell at her indignantly or simply leave the place in consternation? She began to regret coming, for never before had she experienced as now such an oppressive feeling of being a fugitive, above all because the fear that a misplaced look, an inappropriate gesture, might make her suspect in their eyes. It had been crazy to come to such a public place where being naked made her particularly vulnerable. She began sweating and chose instead to close her eyes.

After the apparent interruption, a couple of voices on the other side of Carlos picked up the conversation again.

"All right, tell another one."

"You know the one about the girl who asked her father if she could go to a party with her boyfriend?"

"No."

Antonia heard Carlos muffling a snicker. She opened her eyes and noticed that everyone, including a man shaving at a foggy mirror, was listening to the conversation.

"OK, as papa was a real bastard, he told her she could go but first she'd have to give him a blowjob." The guy telling the joke, a man so fat he had dimples in his cheeks, paused to make sure everyone was waiting for him to go on.

"And?"

"The girl didn't want to, but being late to meet her boyfriend she agreed."

"So then?"

"He dropped his pants and took out his dick. You can imagine the look of pleasure on the guy's face. But just as the girl was about to take it in her mouth, she said, 'Hey, papa, this cock smells like shit.'"

An old man facing Antonia impatiently scratched his member through his towel. She noticed the others were also waiting with interest for the punch line. The man telling the joke laughed, making the dimples on his face stand out even more.

"Then," he finally went on, "her father said, 'Well, what do you want? Your brother just asked to borrow the car…'"

To a great or lesser degree, everyone enjoyed the joke. Antonia found herself pretending to belly laugh when she saw that even Carlos was laughing. Amidst the fog of her astonishment, she discerned in the insolence an act of violent nakedness that compensated for the subterfuges of language and convention like work, neckties, family gatherings. Then it wasn't just a rumor: the boorish world of men could turn so limitless as soon as they found themselves within the limits of a sufficient trust; that is, when just among themselves.

5

To be among only men could also become threatening. Among the naked bodies in the showers a few feigned an indifference that had nothing to do with their urges. Antonia observed that even Carlos snuck a peek out of the corner of his eye at the other men's members. There were so many flaccid penises, all varying in size: did these differences allow one to forecast the loftiness or the meagerness of the erection? Some knew they were being observed, however much the gazes didn't fix directly on the target. The response varied; some became intimidated and scrunched their bodies beneath the weight of a shell, others spread their legs and brought their horns out into the sun. Antonia recalled a similar situation at the urinals, where however much men tried to hide it, they were always looking at their own penises and those of other men in a never-ending comparison and competition. As Carlos in his guise of Alexis would say later, "Whoever tells you different is either lying or fooling himself. We're always trying to see whose is bigger."

For what she could see Carlos was pretty well endowed. Despite the years, his body continued smiling with a joviality that awoke admiration and even envy, as Antonia witnessed in the attitude of respect or rejection stirred in other men. As if there in that skin which guarded muscles, guts and organs were engraved, without conflict, the tracks of a life perceived as full and contented. Antonia began to feel nervous. Why did nudity or the hint of it always end up so disturbing? We are bodies imprisoned by our minds. Only when desire opens the way—Antonia looked with delight at the back and ass of Carlos covered by a layer of suds—do we blossom. She was just about to go up to him when she was seized by fear. And what if he rejected her? Was her desire right? Did the outer change modify her feelings? She was naked but felt the weight of the armor, more imprisoning than protective. She was so lost in thought that she hadn't noticed a young man had been looking at her for a while. She didn't know how or why, it was a long and perhaps eternal gaze, but the boy recognized her and smiled. Antonia responded feeling disturbed and then turned her back to him.

6

To persist but at the same time resist in the wrong terms…Antonia recognized that instead of hunting them, she was confronting women as if both were entrants in a tournament. Far from remaining among the spectators, they also put on armor and attacked the opponent. Antonia had been a woman and anybody would have thought that the secrets and mysteries had already been revealed to her, but the roles of courtship were not distributed so clearly. More than the ladylike rules of corsets and starched petticoats, the joker shook his rattle and made a cut or an opening where there appeared to be no folds: there was always something rather fascinating and unique, as if happiness (Malva smiled while she sat down beside her in the movie theater) or tenderness (Claudia seemed not to understand and insisted on coming close like a panther, sometimes ferocious and other times tamed) were events always experienced as if for the first time.

And although the codes weren't clear—with contradictions in the practices of Casanova, Don Juan and Ovid coming out of the mouth of Carlos, who had followed their teachings ever since adolescence—what's certain is that Antonia was attracted by the fight, by exposing herself, because a desire stronger than herself was pushing her to fill that suit of a man she was now wearing. She didn't want to fall into the easy game of assigning to her present condition this new delight in adventure, but she recognized that her capacity for taking risks without considering the consequences had increased. Maybe that was due to the permissive sensation of her dreams (how else to explain the edges and canyons her life was leading her through now?), but a kind of galloping fearlessness encouraged and moved her to try new things.

There was no other reason for accepting Claudia's invitation to her apartment. Malva had decided to go with Raimundo after the four of them went to the movies and out to eat. Antonia and Claudia fooled around along the way: they'd had a couple of drinks at dinner and Antonia dared to touch her breasts and Claudia slipped her hand between his legs while they listened to Leonard Cohen. And so the cards had been dealt—endless kissing in the elevator—when they arrived to Claudia's place.

But then—they were sprawled on the couch in the living room—Claudia put aside her panther pose and, surprisingly, left the burden of action to Antonia. Still, waiting, Claudia suddenly turned into the very image of the Desire that must be fulfilled. Antonia imagined her as an enormous open mouth, an unfathomed grotto that never—and so absolute do we perceive passion in an instant—never could be satisfied...And she felt terrified, the fear reflected in the dismay of her member, seconds earlier gloriously erect like a flagpole. While it weakened more and more, Antonia began to perceive that the armor of other occasions was being reinforced around her half-naked body. She began getting dressed as Claudia looked on stunned.

"What's going on?" the girl asked, still not quite understanding.

Antonia remained silent. A whirlwind of anger and shame pierced her chest. She didn't even know how it occurred to go on the attack: "You just don't turn me on very much."

Claudia couldn't believe what she was hearing. "Wait," she said while also putting on her clothes. "You can't get a hard on and it's my fault?"

Antonia couldn't listen any more. She left the apartment, slamming the door, but deep inside she knew that this disproportionate boasting—along with her clothes, she'd also put on the coat and breeches of mail so hastily that her bones were about to hit the floor—was an attempt to stifle a squeaking little voice that was crushing her: "You can't, you can't..."

7

Hard armor is constructed to protect a soft weapon. An appendage powerful in its vigor but vulnerable when at rest that doesn't obey your will. It doesn't depend upon you. On the contrary, you are its servant and its power is such that you gravitate according to the object of its desire. Something that Carlos defined as the "gravitation of the gaze": that magnetic inertia that makes your eyes follow a pair of legs, an ass, a strut, without restraining either your will or conscience.

"What's curious is that some men are ashamed they can't control it. I love it, but out of respect to the person I happen to be with I try not being too obvious. But I like it because it makes me aware of my animal nature that responds to the stimulus of a beautiful body, or one of its marvelous parts."

It was dawn and they were on the Plaza Garibaldi, just coming out of a bar where they'd gone after stopping in a few cantinas. Antonia was really feeling down after the episode with Claudia, and rather than cheering her up the alcohol just tapped into her melancholic side. Although she hadn't said anything to Carlos, he'd guessed in her subdued look that things hadn't turned out very well. Out of solidarity he insisted they go out that night, taking advantage of his not having to fly until the weekend. Nearby, groups of mariachis offering serenades tried to approach the few cars driving down the avenue. Suddenly a pair of newlyweds got out of a car. He in his tuxedo and she in her white dress and long train walked through the plaza to one of the bars still open at that hour. A group of mariachis followed, playing snatches of melodies. Antonia recognized several songs, but when the newlyweds finally entered a nightclub, far from stopping the mariachis continued playing "El Rey." The final stanza, "I have neither throne nor queen, and nobody who understands me, but still I'm the king," dragged an ironic smile out of her. She, too, felt like a conquered king, however much she might have boasted about faking the opposite. It was called pride, wounded vanity. But it was doubled because Antonia knew that her behavior with Claudia came from her own insecurity, her unwillingness to recognize that there before her she was, doubly, less a man.

She looked at Carlos looking at her and wondered if he'd ever experienced anything similar; if he'd ever had to hide his own fear by attacking and making his adversary responsible; if, in a word, he'd been just as big a coward. She would have liked to ask him, but instead (don't forget they'd had quite a bit to drink and that in similar circumstances people do absurd things), she started to laugh out loud.

Carlos joined in for a few seconds in a duo of senseless laughing, but finally asked what was up. Antonia had to take a deep breath but then doubled over again in laughter and tried several times to contain herself before able to explain.

"I was just asking myself what I'd be without a penis. If instead of being what I am now I was a woman and, let's say, was named Antonia."

"If you were named Antonia we wouldn't be here. Maybe we'd be in bed together, but this complicity, this company with no threat between us, I've experienced with a woman very few times."

They were both quiet a few moments. A luminous penumbra began to filter from beyond the buildings surrounding them. Day was breaking.

"As well, I couldn't imagine myself without a penis. Maybe it's a matter of the over-discussed castration complex that might be so bruising that I can only conceive of it in a symbolic, abstract way. I know men and women who limit themselves, prohibit themselves things not because they can't be done or undone, but rather by denying themselves, 'castrating' themselves, they think they're avoiding a bigger punishment. But the other, myself, Carlos, without a penis, is a metaphysical transgression...something absolutely irrational. They should ask the Elephant Man how he felt about what was considered human beyond appearances. I would simply cease to be...But well," Carlos finally continued in a low voice, as if afraid to wake someone, "now that Matatías is asleep, I'll tell you about Alexis, another of my personalities. He's the triplet brother of Alex and Alexina; maybe I'll introduce them to you someday. According to Alexis, for us men, and you must be aware of this already, Antón, the fact that our sex organ is exterior is a kind of fundamental confirmation, and so to see it, touch it, show it are necessary, even if unconscious, acts. And that also makes us tremendously vulnerable: there in a pound of flesh is encoded a good part of our humanity. Anyone who tells you differently is lying or fooling himself: it's always a matter of trying to see whose is bigger...For that reason, when it fails you as an amorous lance, it's so difficult to accept defeat. Has it ever failed you?"

The armor wasn't invulnerable. Antonia felt the thrust between two plates and hurried to answer. "Never," she angrily denied to herself.

8

What had so caused her to lie, to keep reinforcing the armor in order to hide her diminishing pride? The truth is she also felt guilty. The next day she went to Claudia's apartment hoping no one was there. She was going to slide a note under the door ("I'm sorry for acting the way I did. Forgive me. It was all a product of my own insecurity...") when she heard someone walking up the steps: it was Malva, wearing a raincoat and an air of vulnerability with which Antonia was already familiar. Still the girl's gaze shone more than normal. Antonia put the note in her pocket.

"Did you come to see Claudia?" asked Malva.

"She's not here..."

"I have keys. If you'd like, we can wait for her."

They went in and Malva took off her raincoat. She was thin and the loose dress she was wearing made her look even more so. She rubbed the tip of her nose with a sleeve in a tender gesture that seemed irresistible to Antonia, who then looked into her teary eyes and felt compelled to ask, "Is something the matter?"

Malva made an effort to maintain her composure but finally sought comfort in Antonia. "I just broke up with Raimundo," she said sobbing.

Antonia couldn't help but think of Casanova and Carlos. Take advantage of the opportunity, take the prey only as far as she would like to be forced. Malva trembled in the arms of Antonia, who all the man was burning with desire: the warrior awoke with an unbeatable force. She no longer knew—nor did it matter that she felt the girl was letting him gain ground—whether such a desire was provoked by Malva or by Antonia's own healed virility.

Penumbra and Photography

1

"Man is the dream of a shadow," Raimundo used to say in explaining the disturbing situations provoked by human behavior. He'd taken the phrase from a poem by Pindar, whom he'd come across while still quite young. The classical Greek poet first caught his attention by reminding him of some of the delirious visions he'd had while unexpectedly ill with the measles as an adolescent. A fever had knocked him flat for days and kept him in a state between watchfulness and dream: "A deeply shadowy zone where reality loses focus of its normal coordinates in order to accommodate a murmuring world inhabited by shadows moving among blurry contours and profiles. In such a trance my mother bringing me a tray of food or the doctor visiting me were nothing more than freely moving reflections: while my mother and the doctor acted with measure and restraint, their shadows had a quarrel that went beyond the comic: at one point the shadow-mother had tried to strangle the shadow-doctor, who in turn could barely free himself and began to hit her with his stethoscope. What's curious is that I saw myself like some sprawling shadow in which only my hands kept their corporality and normal color. With that implacable certainty of dreams, I knew that when my hands fell into shadow I would be dead, but however strange it seems, that didn't make me sad. In other visions the shadows had invaded my room. I got up with an unusual lightness and crossed the room in pursuit of a luminous source of light, a kind of rainbow in the background. It occupied the place where the mirror had been and then, when I peeked into it, I found myself and the room reflected as I'd always known them. I tried to bring forward my gray, contoured fingers and there appeared duplicated other fingers in a vast chromatic scale, but as soon as I moved my hand away and brought it towards other objects, I discovered an unusual feeling of power: I was I and at the same time all the other outlines that my shadow embraced. And while they melted away, I perceived a murmur, a tenuous vibration that each object seemed to exhale.

"I never knew afterwards if it was a dream or had really taken place. One afternoon I got a visit from a friend from high school. Her blue uniform was an isle of light surrounded by shadows, and when I stretched my arm toward her I felt completely moved, because by touching her I could feel that I was taking possession of the sounds of her body, the snapping of her tongue—she was chewing gum—the fragrance from between her legs. But moreover, I discovered that my friend Leylha, that was her name, was at that moment humming a carrousel tune.

"I think amidst the stupor that still had me in its grasp I asked her something about it. A bit startled, Leylha confided in a whisper, 'That's because today I played hooky. We rode a carrousel,' adding with a timid smile, 'I really like merry-go-rounds. I know they're for kids, but don't tell anyone.'

"When I finally got better, I saw Leylha from time to time but I never said anything. It took a lot of effort to resume my normal activities, above all while I was recuperating. At times the edge of a shadow, a silhouette sketched in movement by headlights, brought back to me the shreds of that undetermined zone. I didn't talk about it with anyone back then, but I've always remembered that first passage and the invasion of Penumbria, as years later I named that undefined and powerful kingdom of shadows.

"Throughout my life I've had the opportunity for other encounters. Books, photos, movies, paintings, streets, rooms have persistently revealed to me veiled messages, moments of revelation when things were surprisingly framed in a strange and palpitating beauty, like a secret heart. It's not so strange that a few years after having the measles I chose photography. I clearly recall the day my father decided to leave my mother, my two brothers, and me with no explanation. I was sixteen and went into my father's office to ascertain the things he'd left behind: his pipe, his accounting files, a camera he rarely used.

"With the camera strapped over my shoulder, I immersed myself in the downtown streets. I took random pictures, not paying much attention to the objects captured. I stumbled across a used bookshop and walked through the labyrinth of books without looking for anything special. Tired, I was on my way out when I came across a rather peculiar edition. On the cover the shadow of a woman drew with her finger the nascent, still unfinished body of a man. I opened the book and came across that phrase by Pindar. Then I realized something that in some way I already had known about my father: his shadows were now guiding him down new paths. I bought the book. Of course it was a book of photographs."

2

"So it doesn't bother you if I go out with Malva?" Antonia asked after a few minutes of silence, having listened to the story of Raimundo's fevers, the abandonment by his father, the tale of Penumbria and the phrase of Pindar which, however contradictory it may seem, she understood without really understanding.

"No…in fact you take care of a problem for me. Like most

women, Malva is very demanding. And as for demands and requests, I have enough with my shadows and photography. Besides, the woman hasn't been born who could come between me and a friend."

They'd been developing negatives in the dark room all morning, and while they waited for the last prints to dry, they went out onto the balcony of Raimundo's apartment to have a smoke and take a break. Antonia still held before her eyes the emerging image of a urinal she had taken at the Palace of Fine Arts. Lubricated on the bottom edge by the flash, the urinal insinuated the labia of a pubis, eagerly awaiting to be taken.

She hadn't been able to stop her whole body from trembling as the images began emerging from the chemicals. Raimundo also seemed disturbed by the photo.

"It's marvelous. But you shouldn't forget, Antón, it's a gift from the shadows. Photography is the encounter between a shadow and the possibility of being, the instant when it ceases to be undetermined and unformed in order to become illuminated and acquire body and definition. For that reason shadows are always desiring entities. When we so desire, we become shadows. Shadows of desire. When did you start to desire Malva?"

"The first time I saw her," Antonia confessed in a whisper. "She seemed so fragile and helpless that I felt like taking her right then, to cherish and shelter her. I don't know why but I thought her pussy must have been like a little girl's. Well, in fact it is, because she shaves it."

Antonia looked at the tree-lined street spread out at her feet. It was a cool, clear autumn afternoon. Among the trees she thought she saw one with big white flowers. Yes, it was a magnolia tree. She didn't understand why, but the urinals and Malva reminded her of the shape of those white flowers, immense as the desire they awakened in her. She was about to say that to Raimundo, when out of the corner of her eye she discerned a sudden movement coming at her face. She turned away instinctively and Raimundo's arm remained suspended in the air with a fist that quickly opened in the subtle gesture of a magician releasing a dove.

"What do you want?" the photographer finally asked, adjusting the collar on Antonia's shirt. "It's not me who's jealous. It was my shadow." And he broke out into a laugh that seemed genuine and mischievous, all the more genuine for how much it appealed to her complicity, all the more mischievous for how much she perceived it was the necessary lie—as she now could understand and share the motives—of a knight to save his wounded pride.

3

How was it that she lost herself in her own desire? In a shipwreck the boat is sunk or destroyed by the violence of the elements and, nevertheless, the survivors, those who don't perish, are called the shipwrecked. Now she was shipwrecked by a woman. Shipwrecked by Malva. And it was because when she held Malva in her arms, trembling like a freshly cut blossom, she felt that more than lord and master she was losing herself and abandoning herself, that all of him was melting into a dragging force that impelled him forward to throw herself into the sea, to relinquish who she was and wasn't, to relinquish all doubts, and all certainties, and make way with a raised arm, a heart split apart, and a singing cock.

4

But the issue of Penumbria turned out to be much more important for Raimundo than Antonia thought at first glance. Suddenly the pieces started falling into place: the marionettes of the Javanese shadow theater that presided over the décor of his apartment's living room, the reproductions of famous photos that lined the corridor leading to his dark room, like the one in which the artist Claude Monet had captured his own shadow reflected in a pool of water lilies, or in the unusual self-portrait of André Kertész where one can appreciate his shadowy profile in the act of photographing himself along with the shadow of the tripod and camera...They were images where only the shadows appeared as subjects and the bodies, outside the frame, remained in shadow...To this had to be added Raimundo Ventura's own work, some of which formed part of the collection of the Centro de la Imagen in Mexico City and the International Photography Center in New York. Antonia had only seen the most recent series: photos of a singular beauty where faces and bodies were shown in their transition to shadows, not only by the invasive penumbra of the spaces, but rather because in them transpired pure, thirsty passions: the innocence of being put into the revealing light of an implacable eye. Translucent, with a luminous and brilliant halo, radiating a concentrated and crystalline force, the people and objects photographed by Raimundo Ventura seemed to rip a hidden veil and appear at times with an inciting shyness, at times without pity.

On an altar that Raimundo had set up in one of the bedrooms, an image of the Souls of Purgatory stood out among various photos and portraits. In the center was a vessel where burned a wick floating in oil that the photographer always took care to feed. Every morning Raimundo went there to ask for the protection of his shadows, and when he was working on a particular project to ask them permission to work, invoking with a sort of prayer a phrase that, written in silver ink, slithered upon a piece of paper at the base of the Souls: "Let me be a shadow in your hands."

The first time Antonia saw the altar she felt touched by those words whose meaning she didn't fully grasp. A few steps away Raimundo discerned her interest in the phrase and felt prompted to explain its origin.

"It's the prayer penitents in Java invoke when, tired of life not fulfilling their dreams, they discover in submission true happiness. Doesn't that seem marvelous, Antón? When I start a new project, when I go out into the world with my camera, when I begin a new relationship, I repeat no other phrase than that."

"To leave desire aside?" asked Antonia.

"On the contrary, to allow the desires of your shadows to invade you. Besides, there's no other possibility. You think you hold the reins of your life, but haven't you ever felt that some unknown desire imposed itself upon you?"

Antonia couldn't stop pondering Raimundo's words. Was it possible that the metamorphosis that had her living in the body of a man was due to the power of the shadows?

"Penumbria is everywhere, Antón, and it only takes a murmur for the veils to be lifted and a ray of…darkness…to filter in."

They left the room of the altar and went to the studio. Raimundo brought out a portfolio of work and showed her a serigraph of a poster where the Holy Child of Atocha emerged victoriously from the silvery ink of the background.

"A few years ago I had a show in Madrid of a series entitled 'License to Work.' I didn't know anything then about the Javanese prayer, but read what I put below.

Antonia went up to the table and read the lower part of the poster:

*Little Silver Eyes**
(Madrid/Velázquez 1995)

This petition I bring: that my shadows grant me
license to work, for the world doesn't do so.
I work for them; and I ask they find me worthy.

If you should think of contemplating the triumph
of the Lonely Shadow
who can be cruel or pitying, accompany me
—shadows among shadows—
during the days of this exhibit.

Antonia remained silent a few moments. Then she turned to the
photographer and said with a smile, "Penumbria hasn't abandoned
you, right?"

"No it hasn't. It's my light," he answered convincingly, smiling, too.

5

Antonia and Malva had just fallen asleep when the phone rang. On
the other side of the line came Raimundo's excited voice.

"Antón, you can't imagine what I've just come across—the
shadow at the origin of your urinals. You have to see it for yourself."

---

*In what might be explained as a collective message of Penumbria, this peti-
tion was published, in more or less the same words on the same date, in a
Buenos Aires newspaper celebrating the exhibit of a photographer who liked
to develop (reveal—that is, to veil again) the power and beauty of his own
shadows, Ricardo Vinós.

Antonia stretched, rousing from sleep, but Malva's naked body lying in the sheets made her reconsider the option of going over to the photographer's apartment.

"What time is it?"

"I have no idea. Wait…a little after 1 a.m. You can wait until later but I'm sure you won't be sorry if you come right now. Come on, just head over. I still have a couple rolls of film to develop and can wait for you."

Antonia hesitated a moment, not wanting to leave Malva alone, but Raimundo's words intrigued her.

"OK. I'll get dressed and be over."

As soon as she hung up, she turned to lie against the girl's side. Instinctively Malva embraced him and kissed his shoulder.

"Malva," Antonia said softly, "I have to go out, but I'll be back soon."

"As long as you're not going to sleep with another woman," she mumbled in a sleepy voice, snuggling under the covers.

She was sleeping so happily, her childish face sweetened by that defenseless air of those bodies adrift in a dream, that Antonia couldn't help but kiss her on the tip of her nose before hurrying to get dressed.

As soon as she came in Raimundo offered her a drink that Antonia immediately turned down.

"You were with Malva, weren't you?" he asked, pouring himself a shot of tequila.

Antonia furrowed her brow. "I thought you wanted to see me about something else."

"Yeah, yeah, the shadow of the urinal. You're right, Antón, it's a real discovery to have thought of the urinal as the soft hips of a woman. Few men would dare point out this similarity and much less recognize a pleasure similar to the amorous encounter while standing before one. All right then, I'm going to show you a clear, certain example and you'll be in my debt."

Raimundo took a long sip of tequila and signaled to Antonia to follow him. They went to his studio, lit only by the lamp on the drawing table. The cone of light came down upon a thick book of photos opened to the middle. Raimundo motioned for Antonia to come forward.

On the paper was the nude body of a woman with her arms raised, her face left in shadow while the contour of her hips and pubis revealed the soft line of a living urinal. Antonia felt like the image was blinding her.

"So the urinal is the shadow of a woman," she said in a soft voice.

"Like you...," pointed out Raimundo from behind.

Antonia felt she'd been discovered. With no time to put on her armor, or at least pull out her sword, she managed to raise her shield and ask, "What are you trying to say?"

"Like you, like everyone...Aren't you even aware, Antón, that we men don't exist? We are the fantasy of women's desire..."

6

Antonia was about to wonder what external forces were moving him, when she suddenly stopped before the Palace of Fine Arts, on her right Malva holding hands after a walk around downtown, and in her chest a galloping desire that rent her apart.

"Are we going in?" asked Malva, her nose and brow furrowing like a child obliged to go to a museum.

Antonia took her hand from the girl's and adjusted the strap of the camera hanging from her other shoulder. "It's not what you think," she added with a mischievous smile.

Malva looked at him intrigued and let herself be led along. Instead of going into the theater, they went around the building and headed to the office of Luis Camacho, the theater's head graphic designer and a friend of Raimundo's who had earlier allowed Antonia to go into the bathrooms of the concert hall and take the first photos of those Fine Arts urinals, recommended by Carlos Díaz, which possessed such an obvious sensuality.

Luck was on their side: Luis had just finished up with the month's programs and posters and so could immediately see them. To Antonia's request for another session except now with a model, the designer, a formal but still jovial type who from the very outset had enjoyed the idea of taking pictures of urinals, accompanied them across the inside lobbies to the restroom.

"All right," he joked with Antonia, "now you owe me two invitations for a drink. Why don't we get together with Raimundo this weekend and go hit some cantinas?" Before closing the door behind them, he asked that they not stay past five o'clock because at that hour the staff began preparing for the evening's performances.

As soon as they were alone in that luxurious space of marble veined in black and white, Malva made out the row of urinals but hesitated to approach them.

"How strange," she said, avoiding to gaze fully at them.

Antonia took out her camera and checked the light. She focused the lens on Malva, still leaning against one of the walls as if she were a little girl forced to do something against her will.

"Why do they seem so strange to you?" asked Antonia, starting to shoot some pictures.

"I don't know, maybe because they seem so unknown, as unknown as those French bidets, which at least are designed so a woman can sit and wash herself without having to bathe completely. On the other hand, urinals are objects from the intimate world of men." She walked over and stood before one. "Designed exclusively for their use. I can't imagine peeing here, I'd get all wet. But you guys, with your mobile little toy…" Suddenly Malva became silent while a surprised look came over her face. "But how peculiar those things are…like…"

Antonia took advantage of the opportunity to shoot Malva and the urinals from various angles, as now when she inclined her profile over the porcelain shell, seeming more like a confused little girl poking around the inside of a wishing well.

"What do they look like, Malva?" asked Antonia without taking her eye from the camera lens.

Malva stayed silent a few moments and suddenly confessed to the camera. "Like women," she murmured as if she'd all at once discovered something forbidden. "Now I know why I find them so disturbing."

And biting her lower lip she stood right next to one. She looked at her own hips and suddenly raised her arms so that her face remained hidden behind the fine sieve of a shadow.

Antonia couldn't help but shudder. Had Malva seen the image Raimundo had shown her just a few days earlier of a naked woman, her face covered by the shadow of her arms and the hips like those of a urinal? Had Raimundo shown it to her and if so were they seeing each other behind Antonia's back? Or was perhaps Malva letting herself be carried away by her shadows, letting herself say words, make gestures, strike attitudes, outline profiles, follow routes traced by a vehement, subterranean chance?

"What do you think, Antón?" she asked, her eyes glittering in the shadowy zone where her face was hidden. "Or maybe it'd be better if I took my clothes off."

"Yeah," murmured Antonia dawning with excitement, becoming one with the voracious hunger of the camera.

"All right, I'll take my clothes off, although I don't like to be photographed in the nude. In exchange you have to grant me a wish."

"Whatever you want."

"I've never seen a man pee in a urinal…"

Antonia set down the camera and went up to one. She didn't know if it was due to the excitement or because Malva was looking at him, and how even more difficult it is to urinate with an erection, but she just couldn't discharge into that porcelain vulva. She was working at it but then Malva, her gaze fixed on his member, began to take off her clothes. All of a sudden, as if she couldn't breathe enough air through her nose, she opened her lips in a gesture of absolute docility. At that moment Antonia recognized that the urinal was also a thirsty mouth. And then she didn't know if she was coming or simply pouring out. The release was so intense and pleasant that she had to lean against the marble.

She closed her eyes and from that deep shadow heard Malva speaking like a shadow behind another shadow.

"I want you to make love to me here," she murmured.

At what moment had Malva heard the rumor of Antonia's desire which led her to urge this scene in the restroom of the Palace of Fine Arts? Antonia's heart beat with only one response: desire, a delirious hunger and thirst that overflowed in order to be satiated. She opened her eyes and contemplated Malva's naked body leaning against the urinal, like a bud within another bud. She felt herself gravitating toward that double gyneceum that was also trembling with desire. She spread its petals and became lost inside it.

7

They went out to the street. Two smiling, loving bodies. Without questions. Only certainties. The sky was a singular brilliant blue. The world slid by with an unusual fluidity. The cars and the people crossing the avenue rehearsed a kind of dance: each one in its place, each thing in its time. Antonia contemplated the beauty radiating from that moment, inadvertent photographs where death and life coupled lovingly, and was surprised: it was the same city as always, with the same disorderly chaos, and still it was enough to step back a bit, with that distant and near gaze of someone sated, to discover in the dizziness the whisper, the secret, the heart of things in one's own chest.

She observed Malva. The euphoria of a little girl just getting off the Ferris wheel: her eyes wild and immense like voracious throats with an unquenchable thirst and insatiable hunger. She felt her loosen her grip and flee like flowing water.

"I just applied for a scholarship to go to graduate school in Barcelona," whistled her feverish voice.

Antonia looked at her fingertips where for a few brief moments happiness had taken refuge. She missed her armor, from a gauntlet that would cover her hand again like a steel skin to the tips of her boots, but above all a hardened cuirass, covering the chest that—beyond gender and genitalia—could become a vulnerable battlefield.

8

"I will open my eyes and the dream will be over. Things will go back to normal. I'm only going to like men and maybe now I can get along better with them. As for women..." Antonia paused. She couldn't fool herself: she'd always liked the bodies of other women. So had she been a lesbian without realizing it? But she also liked men. Carlos, Raimundo, each one in his own special way, just like Malva and Claudia. The world was a vast repertory of possibilities. Certainly ever since she'd had a penis—perhaps it was the alchemy of the hormones resulting in unbridled passions—women attracted her more. And so? More than being a castaway, she felt lost in a labyrinth of contradictory feelings and realized that shipwrecks could also be found on dry land. She'd already spent several days locked away with Malva in her apartment, feeding their body in the nocturnal sun of desire, when Malva in the middle of surrendering turned and said, "This isn't going to work. Why fool ourselves? I love Raimundo."

She dressed, leaving Antonia there dejected, and left the apartment without looking back. It took a long time for Antonia to decide to open her eyes. When she did she realized she was still herself, not because of the presence of a penis but from Malva's stinging, sorrowful absence...And in contrast to Adam she recognized that she was missing more than a rib. Like other times in the past, she had exposed herself and been hurt. The world stopped now in a dull clamor that forced her to retreat within herself, a naked minotaur lost within the labyrinth of its own heart.

(But was it really her own heart that had lost its bearing? Conquered, with no strength to go on, she sunk her face into the pillow. The penumbra she opened her eyes to made her aware of herself as an obscurity a bit denser than the surrounding darkness. She knew that she was alive but felt emptied of all desire. She didn't even know how the words came to her mouth; perhaps it was an unintelligible murmur that had been repeated like an echo inside her for some time and only now surfaced to her lips to make her beg, murmuring, "Let me be a shadow in your hands," because she suddenly knew—by the dark light of the chasms we carry within ourselves—that submission was her real strength.)

A Few Labyrinths

1

It didn't exactly have horns but Antonia called it the Minotaurinal, a farewell gift from Malva before she left for Barcelona. She hadn't received the scholarship and so she convinced her father and grandmother to buy her a plane ticket and send her some money every month, contacted some friends of some friends to ask if they could put her up while she arranged to enroll at the university, or took classes, or saw what she had to do in order not to continue with the same life as always. She preferred to give things a try.

With no other choice but to try, measure, take a chance, Antonia understood but her heart didn't. After being denied permission to talk on the phone with Malva, who lived with her grandmother, Antonia decided to stake out her place until she showed up, thinking that see Malva would finally put an end to things. She came across her walking through the park near her home and couldn't hold back. Antonia ran towards her, not caring she was with some friends. Just a few steps away, joking with the other girls and not paying attention to who it was, Malva slowed her step. She hesitated a moment and was going to keep going when she saw Antonia's anxious, fevered face. She opted to say goodbye to her friends and waited for Antonia to come up.

"I need you," Antonia said in a small voice.

"I know," answered Malva looking down at her shoe tips. "But what can I do? I don't need you."

Antonia felt a spear in her chest.

"Can't we please go to my apartment and…get naked?"

Malva firmly shook her head no.

"Not to make love…I just want to touch you, hold you. To feel there's no threat between us. That your closeness can cure me of all pain."

"I'm leaving for Barcelona next week. The truth is I'm really busy getting ready."

"I know…Raimundo told me." Antonia thought she wouldn't be able to stifle her weeping. She felt so vulnerable that she didn't care if that seemed rather improper for a man.

Malva looked at him with rage and pain commingled.

"Ay. I can't stand to see a man cry. It defeats me. It disarms me. Why of all the men in the world do I always get the biggest criers?" exclaimed Malva while she put her arms around his shoulders.

Antonia took a gulp of air as if she were being rescued at the last moment. She felt a spasm so intense that only for that reason did she not burst out crying. Malva caressed his hair and said complaisantly, "You know, at times we wish you men were…different. A bit of violence, jealousy, vehemence wouldn't be so bad."

Perplexed, Antonia broke away from the girl. As a woman it never would have occurred to her to wonder whether that had happened: the desire to be submitted to the domination and power of the other. "It'd really work?" she asked, a bit moved. "I mean…if I could prove that I could dominate you, you'd come back to me, you'd cancel your trip to Barcelona?"

"Of course not, you dummy," Malva replied playfully. "But it would have been nice to see you and Raimundo fight over me."

Antonia moved away from the girl's embrace. She had looked for her, exposed herself without armor and Malva had enjoyed hurting him. For a moment she hated Malva and detested her display of power, her strength and victory, laughing about will and desire. There was a tense silence until Malva was moved to say something.

"The truth is I was going to look for you before leaving. You'll see, I have a surprise, a kind of farewell gift. Are you still interested in urinals?"

At Malva's signal, Antonia crossed the narrow corridor separating the men's room from the women's. They'd gone to the offices of the Civil Registrar where Malva had requested a few days earlier a copy of her lost birth certificate which she needed to get a passport. As soon as Antonia stepped over the threshold Malva closed the door and locked it to make sure no other women came in and were scandalized by the presence of some intruder.

Antonia looked around at those startling surroundings; she hadn't imagined entering again the women's restroom, although the idea of being there didn't seem so unacceptable since, before her metamorphosis, they were the only ones with which she was familiar; nevertheless she couldn't but notice how the strange situation where a pair of doors—in this instance one with the picture of a pipe and the other with a picture of a fan—could subdue her. She recalled how it hadn't been so long ago, just a couple months earlier, when in company of Francisco she had first sneaked into the men's room of some cantina and had run face-to-face into a line of urinals that silently voiced sphinx-like questions that she didn't tire of asking herself: "Who are you and what are you doing here?"

Instead she was sneaking into the women's bathroom now and it seemed she was doubly a fugitive, skating on the uncertain terrain of the transient, slipping along the borders, without a defined place. That terrorized him but also excited her. She looked out of the corner of her eye at Malva to see if he'd been caught. The girl had the brilliant gaze—dizzy and challenging— of someone who has voluntarily become the accomplice of something forbidden. She pointed out to Antonia a peculiar object, built into the mosaic wall, covered with a black garbage bag and sealed with tape.

"This is my gift, Antón: a covered urinal in what must have been going to be a men's room, but is now a women's..."

Antonia noticed then the eyeless mask covering the urinal, which made it appear much more disturbing than if they'd just left it there uncovered. The dark plastic obscured its details, hid its wounding identity, its accusing gaze that revealed a world to which only men had possessed access and which seemingly they wanted to keep sheltered. But would it be so dangerous now for women to visit this bathroom, or was it the result of some masculine modesty that saw at risk an intimacy that should expose neither itself nor men? The plastic tape seemed to gag that object from shouting out. Antonia would have liked to break its bindings to ask about its hidden secrets. But she dared not touch it. Instead she took a couple of steps back and discovered a row of tiles a different color than the rest of the wall, creating what seemed a set of horns above the veiled face.

"It even seems like they did it on purpose: covering the urinal and creating the head of a Minotaur," she said softly, unable to take her fevered gaze from the object. "Who'd ever have thought of that? A Minotaur-urinal in the women's room. A Minotaurinal."

"A what?" asked Malva.

Antonia let out a sigh. It was more than a play on words, but how could she explain to Malva the twists and turns of something that she herself was just coming to discover?

Someone knocked on the door: Antonia and Malva exchanged a frightened glance. After hesitating few moments, Antonia took refuge in one of those individual stalls she used to use, while Malva headed to the door and opened it. Without paying any attention to the older woman who'd knocked and now looked at her with a raised eyebrow, Malva went off down the hallway without waiting for Antonia to come out: in the end, she'd already given him her gift.

2

"WE'RE ALL FUCKING COOL," shouted the graffiti on the tile wall where a urinal was attached in the men's room at the Chopo Museum. Francisco had told Antonia about it and she went there to take some photos.

After Malva left, Antonia hid in the labyrinth for days without answering the phone or even staring out the window. Her body and soul were so exhausted that the suit of armor was left rusted in a corner of the living room. She stayed beneath the sheets until she tired of her own self-pity. She had to have some fun, go out into the world, see friends.

She thought of dedicating herself to the matter of the urinals, for nothing else but those objects so allowed her to discern that limiting dimension where her shadows and most secret desires had placed her. She wanted to see what had been studied on the theme and went to the National Library. She found books on bathrooms and the aesthetics of waste but nothing in particular on urinals. It seemed incredible that at the beginning of a new century and a new millennium, where so many objects of daily life had been subjected to the morbid gaze of researchers, urinals remained hidden in that protective penumbra of the intentionally invisible, of that which had yet to be explored with the forensic instruments of reason.

After searching for a few days she finally stumbled across an 1888 catalogue of the New York fountain-making firm of Mott, sleeping on the shelves of some historical archive, that devoted a dozen pages to displaying urinals. Before her eyes appeared the epoch's stylized and innovative forms, flush systems that guaranteed the elimination of impurities and foul odors, multiple designs that took advantage of space to afford a relative privacy. But what most caught her attention were a few folding urinals, "inoffensive to the view," according to the explanatory phrase found at the bottom of that section of illustrations.

Antonia couldn't stop wondering about the why of that sudden modesty when the act of peeing standing up seemed more a display of arrogance and power, capable of reaffirming virility in its most primary forms, just as the graffiti at the museum exclaimed in that silent scream of victory. "We're all fucking cool," she repeated, recalling a conversation between her brothers that she'd overheard as a little girl, hiding in a closet, about a competition in the school bathroom to see who could launch a stream of piss the farthest into the urinal. Back then Antonia couldn't understand how much pride there was in peeing standing up, but through the words of her brothers who had managed to avoid any ignominy, she understood the burden of infamy and shame the loser had to put up with when, to mark his defeat, they made him sit down on the toilet and pee "like an old lady."*

But on the other hand, this modesty was undeniable, for how else to explain the mask of the Minotaurinal at the Civil Registry she'd seen in company of Malva. Was this modesty, Antonia wondered, the reason why there were urinals only in public bathrooms? Because even if women could always complain about the male carelessness of peeing on the toilet seat (according to Newton's unappealable Fifth Law of Displacement, known within the atmosphere of a joking masculine physics and defined by Carlos, who was surprised that Antonia still hadn't encountered it, as "the harder you try, the more a drop falls out of place"), what's certain is that urinals are never found in a home nor any place in the realm of one's private life. As if it were necessary to remove that other ever vigilant gaze of women from a territorially masculine universe of instinctive intimacy.

"We're all fucking cool," recalled Antonia with a mischievous, almost complicit smile, now that she found herself at home in the bathroom with her zipper down, ready to pee standing up at the toilet. She contemplated the stream of piss stirring up the waters while she weighed the load of the member in her hand. She recognized

---

*One must not forget that the forms and rites of virility are cultural questions: the Arabs urinate squatting because, it seems, they want to imitate the Prophet Mohammed. This was also a traditional position among the Japanese. And so the narcissism of pissing standing up comes from the West. "And the Eskimos, and the Africans?" Antonia asks me curiously. "Leave that to the anthropologists," I respond, attacking her preemptively, "I'm writing a novel, not a sociological study."

that although limp, her penis was of more than acceptable dimensions and she congratulated herself that the nature of her metamorphosis had been so favorable. "They can claim that size doesn't matter, but what peace of mind to go through life knowing you're so well-armed, that at least in that way you're not so vulnerable," thought Antonia to cheer herself up, and then added in jest, "Well, it's always a consolation to know that if worse comes to worse I could get a job in porn..." When she finished, despite her care a few drops marked the edge of the toilet, and she could only consider with a bit of humor the inexorable Fifth Law of Newton. While she wiped up the liquid traces with a piece of toilet paper, she thought, decidedly, that homes should indeed have urinals. She flushed and the whirlpool of water took away the remains in a mechanical, dislodging act. Not even a month had gone by since Malva's departure, but some regenerative vitality—a kind of impetuous discharge that aroused her from head to toe—made him think that perhaps it was time to leave the past behind.

3

To leave the past behind. It seemed so incredible to do so with neither hate nor guilt, without some long, mournful process. Not to get unnecessarily tangled up in things; better just to clean the slate, *tourner la page.* She'd always envied that capacity not exclusive to but notable in men to settle and be done with what they'd lived through. She recalled previous boyfriends, especially Eduardo, who a few months after their separation had written from Brazil to say that he was living there and had married literally a girl from Ipanema, and she concluded that at least in her case, Freud had been wrong: not penis envy, but a yearning for the masculine aptitude for forgetfulness, that nomad's instinct for peeing, zipping up, taking off and being on their way again, while women were left behind to concentrate, tied to memory, incubating resentments, children, hopes…

On the other hand she now felt the force impelling him to change and didn't want to stop to inquire if it came from her actual condition or by the fantasy that now, being a man, was part of him by nature. In any case she decided to enjoy that impulse of liberality as a kind of grace that allowed living the immediacy of the present, to feel light enough to jump from branch to branch or sit there quietly, depending on the whim. It became so clear that nothing was forever that she could feel all that tragic weight she used to carry around being lifted from her shoulders and so went to look for Carlos. The pilot greeted him with a hug and confided he'd arrived at just the right moment: there were plans with Raimundo and Fernando that evening to go out on the prowl and ultimately hit a strip club. Antonia agreed without a word, having never been to one. Well, life went on.

4

(The life that goes on or the steps that trace a road. But first come chance and uncertainty, even though in the end we conclude that we have walked down invisible corridors, designed by a hidden, capricious will that weaves the threads and warps the encounters. Not because we can't escape, but so we can believe we don't desire to do so: on the way over to Carlos's apartment, Antonia discovered near the sidewalk a magnolia tree just a bit taller than he was. She smiled at it because she could now greet it face to face and contemplate the large petals of its flowers without painfully recalling Malva. It wasn't a very busy street so she could pause without worrying about being imposed upon by strange gazes. She went up to smell a flower—a penetrating pubescence—and suddenly knew her love for Malva had been the flower of a day, while the magnolia of desire still cast its scent into the air, renewing itself in an incessant, perennial cascade. Of course she wanted to believe that the encounter was a favorable sign in her labyrinth.)

5

She recalled everything in a fog and could well believe it was only a dream. Voluptuous shreds ripped her consciousness amidst the bad hung-over feeling. She'd drunk too much. The others as well. Antonia's mind was a tumultuous swell that still moved in a gentle and continuous way. It settled on certain scenes that in her mind's eye were repeated, but only to a certain point, stopping just where a kind of discomfort burned parts of her inner skin that cramped in the face of sudden signs of caution and danger. Then it weakened and came back. The sea recoiled to form another gentle wave: the undulating bodies of women that stripped off their clothes to the rhythm of the music, the clamor and whistles of a crowd frantic to reach a visual copulation, as if the gaze were consummated in the progressive nudity of those bodies acting out the fantasy of a gang rape. Antonia could recall the satisfied faces of several of those women who knew they were the masters and ladies of that masculine world which hung on their smallest movements and responded with a collective animalism that subverted the submission: inaccessible atop the stage, vulnerable in their nakedness, the girls exercised the absolute, tyrannical power of desire.

That's what Antonia was thinking half-heartedly because something in her had quickly identified with Carlos, Francisco and Raimundo, who was sunk self-absorbed into his chair, and even with the entire pack of men at the other tables gesturing excitedly, that part of herself until then unknown which couldn't discern things any other way except through the bore of a tunnel where only the will of instinct shone. And now, evoking it here amidst the foggy lack of sleep, in the waves that mounted as the images intensified, this other tangential gaze of hers also converged, a gaze that discovered the desire in others, that allowed her to take distance and contemplate the train, gleaming and rapid, that moved down a long and irreversible, track however much it might stop expectantly at a certain moment, when the lights dimmed and a change in music announced a new act that evening.

Then Antonia's dozing became a detour: for example, she lingered upon those moments prior to the dilated but quite white culmination of a pubis finally exposed and the simultaneous anguish of the glass of vodka on the lips of Carlos; or the threat of a fight provoked by Francisco who'd unintentionally spilled his drink on the pants of the customer next to him.

Anyways she would leave all that for later, although she continued in clear detour, installed in an ebb of peripheral waves while within herself the sea roiled secretly with its oceanic murmur, but then, emerging from the waves and by the force of applause and steady shouts, came the image of the evening's most desired woman: compared to the others who were slutty, elastic, blown-up, spectacular, she was subtly feminine because her body didn't abound in exuberant rounded forms but instead had something unusual about her: she radiated sweetness, the warm promise of an unthreatening contact and intimacy: the seduction that doesn't hide the saber that will behead the St. John the Baptist in each one of them, but—Antonia swallowed in one gulp all the spit that had collected in her throat—the splendor of unconditional Surrender, that promised land, that paradise from which almost all of us have been expelled.

But the oceanic murmur went on. Antonia could swim on the surface, let herself be carried upon the meek and caressing waves of the memory of Tamara, that exceedingly sweet, graceful woman who yanked real howls from the audience as she took off her garb of a shy secretary, or dare dive a bit deeper, spy upon that zone where a diffuse and enveloping penumbra hid—Antonia took a gulp of air before plunging in—the formless, incandescent magma of excitement. Yes, it was there beneath, boiling, obstinate like the resonating echo of the burning breath of the sea. But before her eyes adjusted to the tenuous light—as had happened when they'd gone into the private room they'd paid for upon the insistence of Carlos, where one of the strippers who had been out on stage awaited them—Antonia decided to crawl again to the surface illuminated by the lights of the walkway in order to re-encounter a certain Tamara who, with her blouse unbuttoned, her hair still up, wearing glasses on the tip of her nose, was sliding her miniskirt down over her hips while the lace of the garters, the little panties, and the black stockings worked their lubricious, inciting magic. Antonia could keep enjoying Tamara's body, which started to strut through her memory and radiantly emerge with each garment taken off, until only the glasses and little panties remained—and there again was the feverish palpitation and the stabbing sensation that gave him such a hard-on—but at the same time the deep waters challenged her to submerge herself in the deep shadows of the private room, towards another body that let itself be touched and fondled, palpitated and penetrated—first the tongue, then the fingers, or the other way around, never mind the exact order—by three men, Antonia among them because Raimundo had preferred to hang back and become more of a shadow than the room itself could impose upon him.

Fevered, carried along by the dizzying force that impelled her on, she touched that woman and her fondling hands bumped into those of Carlos and Francisco and then they found themselves body to body, although the objective was something else: that other woman who without being Tamara was giving herself over completely in a submission that she seemed rather to enjoy. Among the flowing images, Antonia would guard the pearly glitter, like iridescent scales scattered haphazardly upon her assaulted body, true winks that pointed to innumerable pleasurable paths.

And Raimundo was observing all this from the amassed power of his shadows, nourishing at will the delay of training his gaze. Antonia knew she was being watched and the waves covered her completely: she lost her breath and tried to rest a few seconds— it couldn't have been longer than that, a few profound moments like unconsciousness—while Carlos or Francisco, or both, did the woman with the pearly glitter. In his corner, Raimundo-shadow finally stood up to join that kind of shadow theater. Antonia was nodding off despite the warning signs. Profiles turned blurry; perhaps Penumbria—through Raimundo's gaze—was opening a path between the bodies. Who was anyone beyond himself? And she fell asleep again, like in the private room, until she felt the eagerness of a pair of lips pressing upon her own. Antonia thought, "The train has entered a deep tunnel." Then she perceived desire as a powerful shadow that invited her to know herself in another way: yes, there was that burning possibility, opened like a fissure's dark, hollow horizon that can take us in unknown directions but at the same time demand that we abandon ourselves to it. She preferred to keep her eyes closed and open herself up to the rails, the waves that with such a caress led her down unexplored inner passages and, for a few moments, disentangled the labyrinth. Then she knew: their bodies were falling into shadow because beyond them shone hidden and blinding, going in the other direction, the thick light of desire.

6

She didn't know why but she remembered the hidden face of the Minotaurinal when the surf tossed her up next to the bodies of Carlos and Francisco, sprawled out in Raimundo's studio among mannequins, advertising maquettes—why yes, the photographer had earlier assured her, my shadows like me to take care of them and they have very expensive tastes. Antonia got up from the couch where she'd spent the rest of the night and stumbled to the bathroom door. She turned the handle and ran into Raimundo shaving in front of the mirror, his torso naked, barefoot, wearing some gray pants. She apologized for the interruption and was about to leave when he gestured her to enter.

"You have to pee? Come in, I'm almost done."

Antonia hesitated a moment but finally stood before the toilet. After all, peeing in front of other men had become more and more natural. Besides, it was comforting to perceive behind her the presence of Raimundo concentrated on the task of shaving. Then she began to pee, inundated by the caress on her lower stomach that made her discharge, loosen up, float. Why not relax if the previous night nothing had really happened? A kiss in the dark didn't mean anything more than a cloaked horseman who was perhaps just worth letting go by. And to feel in his fleeing the absolute disarming nature that mysteries impose upon us. As now she again perceived the horseman's soft touch, this time upon the nape of the neck, then slipping down her back with the silence of light, or should have one said the weightless mass of a shadow? Zipping up and turning around were instantaneous acts but proved useless, for Raimundo had already left the bathroom. She felt disenchanted that they weren't his galloping fingers that had touched her. She had to admit it: Raimundo attracted her with a whirling, obstinate, provoking thirst for shadows. She went to the sink where Raimundo had left his razor and the unclosed can of shaving cream. While she contemplated herself in the mirror, she recalled again the Minotaurinal. She thought that the hidden object could well propose for her an enigma in the labyrinth of uncertainty in which she found herself. She pretended to give voice to it: "What animal is at dawn a flower, at noon a stone, and in the evening has melted into its own shadow?" Or something simpler: "Do you know who you are or why you desire what your desire?" reflected Antonia, a kind of Theseus of her desires, a Desire, Desire-you without a clear path, a dark eel believing itself lost in its own Sargasso Sea, oriented in the right direction by the secret constellation of her shadows without knowing it.

7

(From the Sargasso Sea to the European coasts, a day's run of a 3000 mile-long mobile alphabet, the young eels follow blindly the routes of stellar desire: a gravitation that marks instinct that seals submission/their-mission: As adults they return to spawn in the Sargassos, to go back through the five thousand centuries of the species' frenetic equation. Thus, docile, just being, slippery question marks not looking for any answer, they obsessed the young Freud: four hundred dissected eels in an experimental zoological station in Trieste, a scholarship and dissertation in medicine in order to

85

fascinate himself with their mystery: "No one has ever found the testicles of an adult male eel…" Perhaps, point out his critics in a commentary not exempt from humor, from this seminal failure surged the foundation of the castration complex. Now we know a little better the phases of that mystery—but the prodigy still remains untouched like the long wefts of a hormonal spider web that goes from the Sargasso Sea to the coasts of Europe in a demented coming and going. From the time they are very young, the eels live in the limbo of sexual neutrality from which they then pass on to a paradise of juvenile hermaphroditism before becoming silvery eels and behaving differentially as males and females, but even such definitions conform to the dictates of the environment: levels of salinity, indices of the periodic table of passion. In that blind wandering from one point of the ocean to another, in that somnambulistic happening in which the eels are shadows of instinct, how far will they go not to point out to us some chance circumstance that is as well our own?

And Antonia, dazed by her transformative undulation in underwater currents, unsuspecting of Freud's history, and with absolutely no idea of the sex life of eels, silenced that anguish of not knowing herself and, neither intending it so or preventing it, ended up letting herself by carried off, perhaps because she grasped it couldn't be otherwise, but in reality, to reveal herself, unveil herself, perhaps open herself up to the blow of a secret will that some call chance and others destiny.)

8

(Beyond the fictionally convenient limits, Antonia went to have another table dance. This time she was alone and didn't regret it.

Barely a wink, a tenuous signal and she stopped before the crimson velvet curtains covering the entrance. She noticed then that the façade of the place mimicked the arch of a theater and that up above a marquee announced a peculiar name: "Bambi." It couldn't be the children's film, for that area—one of the routes to Raimundo's apartment—abounded in dives and night clubs. A young man dressed in a suit and no tie came up and coerced him to enter.

"Come on in, sir. The most beautiful women of the evening await you," said the youth while parting the red curtains, letting a whisper of disco music escape from within. Antonia observed the boy's shiny, insistent eyes—it was a Thursday night, almost 10 o'clock, the street appearing rather like an abandoned stage—and almost simultaneously she noticed that one of his fingers was caressing the velvet edge of the curtain, while the rest pulled it back. It was a repetitive, mechanical caress, hypnotic like the smoothness of the cloth and the promise its folds hinted at. She couldn't resist and went in.

Suddenly there was the strident music, the surrounding shadows and the rectangular dance floor, an almost naked woman twirling around a pole in the center, the rain of reddish light that changed shapes upon the open front of her body. Near the edge of the dance floor a thread of empty chairs made possible a prying view at ground level, but Antonia preferred one of the circular seats arranged on a raised tier that gave a wider view of the stage. Full-bodied, with big breasts and a round, firm ass, the woman kept up her improvised dance in front of the place's few clients—Antonia counted people at just two other tables besides her own.

A waiter came over to take her order. Despite imagining the dubious quality of the liquor served there, Antonia asked for a vodka. She needed inside her the violent heat of a strong drink. When she turned her gaze back to the stage she discovered with astonishment that the woman was standing right there dancing for him. Automatically desire shot off as if a wound spring had finally been released. Sweating with excitement, Antonia noticed the woman's chiseled profile: heavily made-up cheekbones, a thin nose, a prominent chin. There was something artificial in her features, the same in the turgid perfection of her tits and ass: an exaggerated desire to please and provoke that was also reflected in the deliberate sinuousness of her movements when she danced. The waiter finally arrived with the vodka. Antonia tossed it down like water. Seen through the bottom of the glass, the image of the woman went a little out of focus. Looking at her again, she realized that in reality the woman wasn't looking at him but was rather dancing for somebody behind Antonia, who feeling confused turned around slightly only to discover his own unshaven face in a mirror that duplicated the space in an unusual way. She observed the woman who strutted to another song while pretending to undo the ties holding up her thong and play with herself, but out of some inexplicable bashfulness didn't dare show her pubic area. From a nearby table where two men hung on each other, flanked by women just like the one on stage, came a whistle and a shout.

"Take it off already, faggot!"

The woman replied with an obscene gesture and paying no more attention to them continued dancing for herself and perhaps for Antonia's reflection, which looked at her surprised, finally noticing her square shoulders, the almost non-existent waist, the small hips, all of which displayed an uncertain crossing of boundaries, the vestiges of a transit from one kingdom to another by the work and grace of plastic surgery and hormones. Oblivious to the effect she caused in others, this woman strutted about and exhibited herself with a body for a disguise. And with the shining gaze in the mirror, contemplating her own rounded silicone forms, she moved, seducing herself, caressing and penetrating herself in desire. Antonia quickly drank down the rest of the vodka while the music stopped and the woman hurried off the stage. After joking a few moments with the guys who had shouted at her, she came up to Antonia smiling.

"Buy me a drink?" she asked flirtatiously.

Antonia remained mute a few moments.

"So then, papacito, those rats got your tongue?" said the woman while she caressed her breasts, offering them up to Antonia's gaze. They were smooth and ended in two tight buds that could barely contain themselves: overflowing in an idiom of murmurs urging to be touched, they stirred hunger. But Antonia hesitated. She thought that however corporal and authentic those breasts seemed, touching them in reality would be like touching a shadow. And since her own transformation had been the product of desires that had worked in shadow and secret, how could she confront, from shadow to shadow, this other transformed body?

"It's just…," mumbled Antonia, desperately hanging on to one of those limits. "You see, I used to be a woman…"

The dancer didn't seem to have heard Antonia's words, which melted into the first chords of a sweet, rhythmic ballad, and she turned her gaze toward the dance floor where one of her colleagues was beginning the ritual anew.

"You know what, little sister?" she finally said so Antonia could hear. "I was a woman, too. Before all this, since the beginning of time, I've always been a woman…" And she let out a playful peal of laughter before heading off with her body baggage to the dressing rooms.

Antonia looked at her empty glass but instead asked for the tab. The new woman on stage, dark and curly-haired, spectacular except for the most upturned nose, as if it had been trimmed down the middle, forced Antonia to ponder the new dimension that the game of life had placed before her eyes: it wasn't some wild fiction, but a reality of incarnated appearance. When she arrived to her dressing room and stood before her own intimacy, would the woman who had been on stage ever ask herself like the urinals asked Antonia in an enigmatic voice, "Who are you and why do you desire what your desire?" No, converted into the very object of her desires, perhaps she wouldn't have to explain anything. Her body was no longer an inquiry, an adventurous sign, but rather a completed reply.

Before leaving, Antonia noticed the image of an entire body repeated in the mirrors off to the side that also enclosed the exit. It was the strange figure of a woman with a curvaceous body and the head of a small doe. Her eyes, as big and gentle as Bambi's, smiled at Antonia with a disconcerting and unexpected complicity.)

9

Sex between men is almost always violent. Antonia had yet to learn that. More than caresses or tenderness there is the imperative of urgency. To jump in and take a gulp of the ocean, to board the train of no return, all conscience focused on movement and friction, the piston of a machine greased to increase its efficiency until melting into the concentrated, expanding universe of a vaporous cloud.

After the episode at Bambi's, Antonia wandered around the area awhile before deciding to knock at Raimundo's apartment. She knew he was home because she could see from the street a light on the third floor balcony and for a few moments the transparent blinds showed a shadow going from one side of the studio to the other. Her steps had finally brought her there, she'd climbed the stairs that separated the street from the building entrance, but her finger remained pensive above the buzzer's curving surface that she caressed with the careful, quiet trajectory of doubt. She went back and forth, unable to decide. It wasn't she who pressed the button in order to continue touching destiny: her finger possessed its own unknown will. Once again she knew that she was at the entrance to the labyrinth with no other choice—having to go in—and with no way back. Despite everything, she wanted to enter.

"Who is it?" Raimundo's voice asked through the intercom.

She heard herself say "Antonia," not understanding exactly what she'd done.

A moment to search out suddenly the possible paths, perhaps a side-long glance that embraced doubt as well as possibility, and Raimundo replied from the other side of the wall, "Come on in. I've been expecting you."

The electric hum extended like a baited line. Antonia fished for it before it went out and she pushed on the door with her whole body.

Getting off the elevator she turned right as on other occasions. Nevertheless, this time her hand slid along the wall of the hallway as if it wanted to feel the passage itself, the act of entering, of venturing down an unknown slope. The door of the photographer's apartment was ajar and to open it she had only to push lightly with the same finger that had just pressed the buzzer. She continued walking down the corridor with her hand glued to one of the walls, but before reaching the little intersection where she would have to decide whether to go in the living room or turn down the hallway that led to the other bedrooms, Raimundo's voice indicated, "This way." Then Antonia loosened herself from the wall and let herself be guided by the tenuous gleam that came from the living room. She'd just crossed beneath the arch separating one space from the other and her gaze was caught by a peculiar object, placed upon a kind of pedestal, ready to be photographed among crimson curtains and translucent screens that guarded their indifferent florescence. She had to lean again upon one of the walls before she understood what was happening. Was she really in Raimundo's apartment or had she dreamed of entering the photographer's studio and there, unexpectedly, definitively, the flower of a urinal radiated its concentrated and secret glow? Hypnotized, she walked towards it.

"What do you think about the little beast? Beautiful, isn't it? I bought it for you and was thinking about bringing it over to your place but I couldn't resist the pleasure of taking some pictures of it. That's why I left you so many messages on your answering machine: I really wanted you to come see it," said Raimundo all excited from behind her, as exultant as if he were galloping on a horse and had just paused briefly so Antonia could mount.

Antonia stumbled a couple more steps towards the urinal: a heart-shaped bud of used but still vibrant porcelain, it reminded her of a magnolia flower turned inward. She thought, intuited, felt that only for the person who could look at it would this flower open its petals and unfurl its indifferent beauty, and then radiate its desire. And Raimundo, who called it the "little beast" as Antonia had at one moment come up with "Minotaurinal," had been touched by its blind gaze.

"I found it at an antique store…I was sure you'd be fascinated by it," he said in a murmur that Antonia felt burning on the back of her neck. Then Raimundo's hand quivered atop her clothing on her nascent penis. It was his only gentle gesture with Antonia because afterwards everything became hurried in an imperious, tyrannical urgency. To subdue, to conquer the body of another man can be a question of strategy but above all force. Antonia thought of two rams colliding for a sole female; she imagined their horns locked in fury, the crash of those bodies electrified by a lethal instinct. Only this time the opponent and the female (the rival and the prized) melded into one sole body that had to be forced into submission. Then she knew. She knew that sex between men is, above all, violent.

10

Before, when she was a woman, she'd had anal sex, so she knew doubly, triply if we add in a vagina and mouth, what it was to be penetrated. But...perforate another man? She was lying next to Raimundo's body, a few steps from that sort of altar where the urinal taciturnly looked down upon them, when the photographer said, "You know, Antón, despite whatever may have happened or what might happen, I'm not the one you're looking for. You know that, right?"

Antonia remained silent a few moments. Her body was still floating adrift on an unknown but unusually pleasant surf. She had to concentrate to remember why she was there.

"But I don't know what I'm looking for. Sometimes I think I just go into a labyrinth, measuring out in the shadows passages that lead me towards unknown places. It's like the urinals: before I couldn't have imagined that they'd become so important to me. That, in fact, they would mean to me a kind of personal quest. Did I tell you about the one covered in black plastic in a women's room Malva took me to see before leaving for Barcelona which I named the 'Minotaurinal'?"

"No, you didn't said anything to me, but I suppose that refers somehow to do with the Minotaur in Crete, right?" replied Raimundo as he sat up and grabbed a pack of cigarettes resting on the night table. He lit one and taking a puff observed the urinal on the pedestal. "Now...I can perfectly imagine: the crossbreeding of kingdoms, the world of objects that suddenly has a human face that as well could be the hips of a woman. Before knowing you I never noticed urinals. Now I even have an erotic relation with them. They look like mouths, too…"

Antonia looked for Raimundo's face. She recalled the first time she'd seen him and noticed his fleshy lips that at the time she couldn't imagine kissing. Once again desire began to open. She perceived its smell, an intense aroma both acidic and sweet, and felt an electric shiver run quickly through her penis, which arose with that tyrannical will before whose power there was no other option but to surrender.

Raimundo perceived that awakening in the body sprawled beside him and it was as if a growing fire also stirred in him.

"Antón, Antonia, whatever your name is, there are always ways to make your way out of the labyrinth. The simplest is to place a hand on the left wall or the right, but always on the same wall. Perhaps you won't take the shortest route like that, but sooner or later you'll exit the labyrinth," he said, his hand running over the profile of Antonia without touching her. Antonia felt the silhouette of the caress as if the photographer were marking that undefined, uncertain zone where desire was just a nameless awakening.

"So, you know about labyrinths, too…," mused Antonia, suddenly grasping Raimundo's arm. They began to struggle, Raimundo trying to free himself, Antonia grabbing him. It began as a game but increasingly became a strength of wills. Antonia started getting turned on, feeling her body of a man reacting more forcefully the more the other resisted.

"There's just one detail, Antón," said Raimundo, taking a breath. "With the method of the hand upon the wall, it's likely that you'll never get to the center of the labyrinth, that you'll pass beside its inner island and not discover your Minotaur. If you want to come upon the sleeping beast, you'll have to get loose," he said and instead of continuing to fight he lay down beside Antonia.

Sprawled face down, Raimundo was a raft to be boarded to cross new seas. Instead of letting him go, Antonia pinned him down from behind with a violence she didn't think herself capable of. She kept going like that—Raimundo's body defeated, ready—and recognized that she'd never before felt such power: a victorious plenitude, the splendor of a sword with which to subdue and behead the other. To turn him into a shadow with her very own hands.

11

(But then, having let go of the walls and handles, relenting to be carried along by a dragging force that propelled him to probe more and more, she opened her eyes just a bit and saw the diffuse image of the urinal mounted atop the pedestal like a porcelain flower opening before its own splendor. A magnolia with translucent wings that, as soon as it opened them up as widely as possible, began to languidly, then definitively, lose its petals, pale as desire, flower of a single, even if endless, day. Like a penis after coming. And she foresaw, like never before, the shapeless, voracious face of emptiness.)

The Art of Ovid

1

She—because there was no doubt about her sex, although looking at her closely one saw a disconcerting beauty—was poking through the books at Francisco's stall while Antonia watched out of the corner of her eye and let the woman do as she wanted. Francisco was recovering from the flu, so Antonia had spent the whole morning at the little stall and was starting to get bored when she noted her at the top of the stairs leading down to the subway. Just seeing her with that distracted air and sleepwalker's gaze that made her float in a cocoon that nothing nor nobody could touch made Antonia think that desire is never innocent: as soon as it awakens, it plots, schemes, lurks.

She made no sign nor openly looked again at the woman, who was now finally coming towards him. Motionless, fixed on the wonder that the woman stirred, Antonia remained alert, every sense honed to capture the slightest movement of that fleeting presence. There was one moment, after the woman had picked up and put down a book only to take another she leafed through and then abandoned for yet another whose first page she began to read, that she waited expectantly and then Antonia realized that they'd each noticed the other and both knew it. As certain as if the pores of his skin were expanding and he could perceive the body temperature, the smoothness of her cheeks or the suppleness of her back. As full as the aroma given off by her just bathed body that wasn't purely her own but as well mixed with the smell of Antonia's reaction to her. And well, yes, at the same time so tenuous, barely a fragrance of freshly cut lemon that only they could discern. And savor—although they weren't fully aware what they were up to, they had smelled each other, and yes, they liked that part, too. That is, a knowing without knowing that they knew, but far from complete ignorance. Measuring each other in that uncertain approximation where the body is sovereign and sends and receives unarticulated messages.

Then suddenly, without agreeing to it, they looked at each other and couldn't avoid, even if they had tried, breaking into a smile. It was a signal as natural as making way for a child on a bike pedaling down a smooth but undeniable slope. As warm as a sunny room that in a profile of light and shadows lifts its arms and says to us, "Come in, I've been waiting for you…"

In the middle of the smile that had already lasted an eternity, she said, "My name is Paula and I've come to grant you three wishes…"

Antonia was going to say her name as well, but then she reassessed the situation and stopped, hesitating between formulating the first wish and distrusting this crazy woman she'd just met.

Paula let out a little laugh and stated, "Seriously, I'm kidding…" And both, once again agreeing, laughed while the people at the other stalls and those passing by on the way to the subway watched as if these two shared a fever that joined them and separated them, a couple of crazy people. At one moment while laughing Antonia felt that something was dislodging and flowing, something like a torrent of vibrating, glistening eels, and yes, decidedly happy to flow beyond the Sargassos.

2

The Sargasso Sea or a blind passage in the labyrinth, that was her relation with Raimundo. It wasn't that they'd fought or were no longer interested in each other, but certainly desire had faltered. They shared now an interest in urinals, shadows and photography, but that state of grace which seemed like love faded after a few weeks. Once again they were good friends. For that reason, because they had found each other again in that alternative terrain of trust and affection, Antonia didn't hesitate to confide in him the encounter with Paula.

"I met a marvelous woman," she said on the phone while her fingers threw a dart at a target she'd hung on the closet door a few days earlier. Despite her little practice, the throw hit a circle near the center.

"Well, where did you meet her?" asked the voice of Raimundo, who seemed taken by surprise.

"At the bookstall. Fernando was sick this morning, so I had to go and…well, Paula showed up there—she's beautiful, crazy. She's a biologist and works at an institute of archeozoology downtown, although she specializes in biodiversity, and every morning takes the subway and passes by the bookstall. She lives just a couple blocks away and…"

"And she told you all this right after you met? Because you said today, right? You guys must be in a hurry."

Antonia laughed out loud. She'd just tossed another dart and hit the target right in the center. She felt an expansive well-being and added, "Well, that's not all: she also writes short stories and keeps a journal of her dreams. Ah…something else: she asked me to a dinner tonight for her work, I think with a few researchers from the famous Aeolian Islands, part of an exchange program her institute has to do comparative studies of Popocatépetl and Stromboli on the effects of habitat recovery after an eruption. In fact, she's probably going there next summer, so you can see I have to hurry. I just came home to shower and change. But I thought I might talk to you…"

"What? Aren't you even going to introduce me to her?"

"Later, later. I'm not going to let your shadows fall in love with her. I tell you, she's fascinating. As soon as I caught her gaze I went crazy…Yeah, I turned into a crazy bitch, because even as a woman I would have fallen in love with her."

"You're exaggerating."

"You have to meet her, but later…"

"So have a good time…And, well," responded Raimundo after thinking for a few moments, "good luck."

Antonia touched the point of a dart with the tip of her finger, running over the polished steel skin, molding herself to the small, curving surprise of discovering it, before asserting with a voice that not even she herself recognized, "Thanks, but I don't think I'll need it."

3

The metaphoric forces of desire…to peek at them through the keyhole of an unalterable gaze which contemplates from outside what from up close can't be seen inside it, Antonia had to read one of the stories that Paula wrote during those days shortly after they met. The surrender hadn't yet taken place, but rather powerful exchanges in which a refreshing happiness grew that made them walk on air. But days later when it happened, when they had finally both taken off their clothes with every intention and opened their labyrinths in order to find each other, Paula wasn't at all shy about showing her one of those stories—half invented, half even more because fantasy always resides there in the middle—and so Antonia began to read while they lay in bed, their arms and legs all entangled.

"This man awakens my man," Antonia read, unable to keep from blushing.

4

(Story Without a Wolf)

"This man awakens my man. He arrives late to the dinner of researchers to which I've been invited. With no appetite at all, I've barely nibbled on a couple of hors d'oeuvres. He waves and comes to my side through the crowd. He's simply charming. He plays his flute and I undulate to it, coming out of my basket. His smell opens me. We talk without paying attention to anyone else: I recount to him the story about the eels in a book by Cortázar that blindly flow out of their desire, he tells me about the urinals in a bar, Diego's, 'so odorless and clear you could drink the water from them.' Suddenly under the table he puts his hand on my leg. He discovers the bulge that only grows for a few people. 'I didn't know women had penises,' he whispers in my ear. I feel an almost painful pressure between my legs and smile at him because he's also awakened my hunger. A waiter places a platter of cherries and cheese on the table. I take a piece of fruit between my fingers and voraciously begin to devour it. My man gets up and heads to the bathroom. After a few moments of answering numerous questions posed by another guest there, I excuse myself to go to the women's room. I open the wrong door.

"There is my man. He's not surprised to see me but he trembles and blushes with a sudden fever. I go up to him and caress his timid breasts of an enchanted maiden. They finally awaken. I say to him,

'Well, well…they've grown,' and I bend over to suckle them. He eagerly caresses my bulge, hungrier and hungrier. His eyes are now an ardent supplication. Then I order him, 'Turn around.' His hands lean upon the edge of the urinal while I confess to him, 'Now indeed I'm going to eat you up…'"

5

When she finished reading the little story, Antonia turned in the bed until she encountered Paula's body face down. She began to cover her back and ass with jumpy kisses that made the girl giggle and writhe with pleasure. Antonia played at provoking her but knew it was more than a game: a tribute, a rapture, a fascination for that supple, audacious body just on the edge of adolescence, in which a subtle but subjugating sensuality exhaled decisive breaths of desire. Feminine? Masculine? "Let's see, turn around, show me that bulge of yours that only grows for a few," Antonia toyed again, forcing her to roll over. Paula resisted: it was a body provocatively resolute in its ambiguities. She could go from a smile to a frown in an instant. She was a woman but knew how to be a man: in a flash she flipped Antonia over and pinned her to the bed. She opened Antonia's legs and without a second thought gave her an unknown pleasure. Antonia half raised up to look at Paula and for a moment, while the latter closed her eyes and made a sweet expression, like a little girl eagerly eating an ice cream, discerned the irrevocable empire of submission. It was barely an instant, the transit of a shadow before becoming incorporated into the light: Paula opened her eyes and watched him watching her. Antonia felt disarmed: no one had ever before so taken possession of her pleasure. Prostrated before her penis, on her knees but for all that no less powerful, Paula raised herself to make Antonia hesitate on that border where pleasure turned into a precipice: who was subjugating whom?

(It was like the urinals and their super-concentrated solipsism of peevish magnolias: frequently Antonia couldn't urinate into them without thinking about their disposition of mouths blind to the desire they provoked. Nobody had ever given her fellatio, but it seemed that in many of her encounters with urinals the shadow of a similar voluptuousness was drawn: there, in the world of those seemingly inanimate objects, throbbed the breath of an almost voluntary surrender that very few dared recognize. And it was enough to pull back the curtain a bit, to move oneself from the usual position in order to discover in the perpetual narcissism of those objects the reverse of one's own gaze: a fulminating transparency that erases boundaries and makes of us its mirror.

"That is, desire doesn't surge from objects but is in the gaze of the person looking," suggested Paula after Antonia confided her latest observations on the theme of urinals. They were hungry and had started dressing to go out and eat.

"It seems to me you're becoming somewhat fetishistic," continued Paula while buttoning a pair of overalls that made her look like a grown-up little girl. "And the truth is I don't see why, because urinals really are pretty in themselves. As are in reality most things and beings when you look at them with due attention, as my scientific colleagues would say. Now, in order to stay pretty and beautiful and all that, this princess needs to eat. I already told you about my problem with hypoglycemia, no? Where are we going? Why don't you take me to that bar Diego's you told me about?"

"That won't be possible," answered Antonia with feigned pain, "unless, of course, we take a plane to Madrid. No, woman, what I told you about the urinals at Diego's I just imagined. I've never seen them. It was Carlos Díaz, a pilot friend of mine who told me about them. I'll introduce you two…So now you can correct your story with the precise, necessary details…"

"Well, no, my man. Precise details are for biology and its fellow sciences. When one writes, and this was explained to me by my ex-husband, who was, or still is, a famous writer, the least important thing is that something be true—it's enough for it to seem so.")

6

Why was she so obsessed with urinals? If relating them to vaginas could sound perilous, wasn't it then excessive to imagine them as transfigured mouths?* And what about those that descended all the

---

*The idea didn't turn out to be so wild, as Antonia would later confirm, when Miriam Grunstein, one of the few friends she had hung onto from her past life, after learning of the photo project that Antonia was undertaking, sent her a humorous image that had circulated anonymously on the Internet.** The characters, author, and editors of this story thank in advance any information that would allow us to give due credit.

** Shortly before the original edition of this novel was published, Antonia called to tell me about something she'd just read in the newspaper. "They have red lips and upper teeth," was the headline of an article published by EFE news agency which discussed the decision by Virgin Airlines to refrain from installing at JFK Airport, due to criticism by a feminist coalition, urinals with the form of a woman's mouth. According to the article, the polemical urinals, called "Kisses," came from the catalogue of the Dutch firm Bathroom Mania! and are the original creation of designer Meike van Schijndel.

way to the floor, very few of which had a receptive shell? Antonia scratched her head. What's certain is that ever since the day she woke up inhabiting a man's body and had to make use of them, their variety of forms had subjugated her, as if an erotic aura emanated from their hypnotic, crushing vortex. Wherever she went, she sought them out and photographed them. She chose places for the sole fact of discovering new ones. Museums, restaurants, hotels, bars, bus stations. Accompanied by Carlos Díaz and David Lida, a writer from New York who was a friend of the pilot and knew forward and backward the bars and cantinas downtown, they went to a unique pulquería, the 60 Colorado, whose urinal, a metallic trough in view of everyone, was located just a couple steps inside the front entrance. As soon as they stepped through the swinging doors, the urinal rusted by constant use greeted them with a worn-out but frank smile.

"What do you think, Antón?" asked David in fluent Spanish as soon as they sat down at a table near the door. "I pay my debts: I told you it was quite a special urinal, and well, you see…"

Antonia was absolutely amazed. She looked at the trough with its still shiny splashes and it seemed impossible to her that any of the regulars—construction workers, truck drivers, warehousemen from the area—would dare urinate in front of the others in a space that wasn't really a bathroom.

"Here comes the best, when someone here gets up to pee…"

"Something that won't take long," broke in Carlos, looking around. "The clientele looks like it's been drinking for a while. And on that point, what are we having?" Then, in a grandiloquent tone, for it seemed he wasn't interested in faking some anthropological, judicious interest, he asked, "Is there anything besides the disreputable pulque, another sacred beverage now relegated to the lower depths of the most impoverished crossbreeding?"

"Well, Carlos, considering we're in a pulquería…," said David with a condescending smile, pointing out to him the price list behind the counter that also included the famous *curados* made of pulque and fruits in season.

"Well at least…I think I've decided on a guava *curado*…Now that I've been abstaining from guava trees, it doesn't sound bad at all," clarified Carlos with a look of sly seriousness.

"Excuse me, Carlos, but I don't understand," broke in David with a rather friendly tone.

"Can you believe it, Antón, David doesn't know what a 'guava tree' is?"

Antonia couldn't help smiling. She wasn't quite sure either what Carlos was getting at, but she could well imagine: in his kingdom of puns, every one-eyed man had at least two eyes.

"Of course you know what a 'guava tree' is, David. Unless," Antonia took a marked pause, "you don't like women."

"In that case, since my wife is away on a trip," conceded David, playfully gesturing to the waiter to come take their order, "I'll also have the guava 'cure.'"

They'd just been served large glasses with a milky liquid when a middle-aged man got up from a table in back and, in a movement that Antonia perceived in slow motion, ended up standing before the urinal by the entrance. On his way there the man avoided the tables with other regulars who also moved in a slowed time, a sort of sleepiness that blurred the precise limits of daily life with its burdens and suffering, as if the pulque still retained that magic effect for which the Aztecs considered it a drink of the gods. A couple of patrons had frankly given in to the sleepy seduction that annulled the narrowness of their present life, sprawling asleep upon the table with the swollen mask of the almost dead. In that unique space where life erased its limits, like a lewd woman who lifts her skirt above her waist in a public square, the men made toasts and imbibed with a desert-like thirst, they spoke about injustice and loves lost, they slept or consoled each other's bad luck without the least circumspection. Antonia thought then that perhaps feeling each other so close, far now from the shame of knowing themselves individuals with the obligation of protecting a distrustful intimacy, they let themselves be enveloped by that white surf of the Goddess of Pulque, which turned them into brothers sharing a common sorrow. Close by, so many distances now annulled in that strange promiscuity, not one of them flinched when that man who got up from his table and now stood before the trough took his member from pants dusty with cement from the construction site where he worked and, with no hesitation, began to pee in front of everyone.

Antonia glanced at her companions, along with her the only outsiders in that rarified world. Between the puzzlement and the feigned indifference, Carlos and David tried to swim above the situation. Suddenly the concentrated smell of urine, certainly made more intense by the pulque's milky acidity, rose up like a giant wave that took away their breath: a kind of repugnancy, but above all the dizziness of discovering in that promiscuous world of smells a tumultuous sordidness, the multitude of lurking murmurs besieging the skin that force oneself to climb their own highest tower and escape that which is so close to us, warmly foreign.

Antonia felt like she was suffocating and had to rush out of the place as quickly as possible. The others caught up a few seconds later, David having entertained himself a bit more while paying the tab for the glasses they'd barely touched.

"You can't take anything," Carlos scolded her once they were outside.

But Antonia paid no attention to him, absorbed as she was in explaining the confused sensations that she'd just experienced.

They were still walking along the sidewalk packed with stalls and vendors. Despite the waste from construction sites and the garbage accumulating in the gutters, downtown morbidly bustled with unstoppable movement. They finally arrived, thirsty and hungry, to the Gallo de Oro, a genuine cantina typical of the era of Porfirio Díaz, with porcelain urinals reaching to the floor surrounded by Moorish tiles that provoked the fantasy of urinating in an Oriental palace, as Antonia was able to confirm a few minutes later. While they waited for their drinks back at the table, David said to Antonia, "Just for your collection of anecdotes on the theme: during an interview, the filmmaker Jodorowsky mentions a man who used to go into public bathrooms with a slice of bread to dip into…"

"No, David, don't give Antón any rope with more filthy stories."

Antonia smiled before turning to Carlos and asking, "And now who can't take anything?"

And they changed the topic, diving into a discussion about soccer and whether the Pumas could win the championship again after several disappointing seasons. Antonia, aware of her disadvantage talking sports, seemed into it and even ventured a subtle comment to avoid feeling like she was exposing herself. But in reality her mind was somewhere else: the terror—but as well the satisfaction and anxiety—of walking through the muddy terrain of our perversions, above all when the gaze of others has become our own.

7

Francisco looked through the stalls at La Lagunilla, exchanged greetings with the vendors he knew, and pointed out to Paula and Antonia rare editions worth buying.

"Look at this *Dance of Death* with engravings by Holbein… what a little gem."

Paula let go of Antonia's hand to take the book Francisco held out to her. She opened it cautiously and glided her fingers over the yellowing pages, tracing the outlines of the prints and antique typography. The caress of the paper and ink made her smile, as if they were the wing of an angel.

"It really is beautiful," she said, and her smile leapt in an arc toward Francisco, who returned it without thinking. Antonia observed just a few steps away the open-mouthed look on her friend's face, where surprise and fascination were confounded, and she couldn't help but think of herself when she first met Paula at the subway entrance. She recognized that something in her provoked a sweet reaction in those with whom she came in contact, even someone as reticent as Francisco. It seemed she had never before met a person who so subtly but effectively undermined one's defenses and all that protective scaffolding that people are used to constructing in their relations with others. And more than jealous, Antonia was entranced by that state of vulnerable affirmation that a gesture of hers could provoke. In any case, she couldn't resist giving Francisco a nudge before asking, "Did you already forget what we came here looking for?"

Francisco frowned and, rubbing his ribs, cast Antonia a reproachful glance. Paula, who'd figured out what was going on, sympathetically nodded and got ready to ask the vendor before Francisco could.

"We're looking for an anatomy book…by Vesalio. You wouldn't have a copy?"

The bookseller, an obese man with greasy hair pulled back into a long ponytail, gave her a lascivious yet disdainful look and, instead of answering, held his hand out to Paula as if begging for alms. Francisco hurried to quietly break in.

"Why don't you put *Dance of Death* back…"

"What a grouch," said Paula, putting the book back in place.

As they began to leave, Antonia felt a kind of ease: it was good to know that in some way Paula was as mortal as everyone else, that she could also provoke resistance, disgust, even open hostility.

They ended up giving someone Francisco knew the task of looking for the book. In any event, they kept wandering around the flea market stalls where invisible hands seemed to work secretly upon the arrangement and layout, bringing close an apparently incongruous collection of things. More than once the three winked at each other before that kind of surrealist installation that haphazardly surprised them at every step. Two things in particular caught their attention: a toilet made into a pot from which sprouted the long shoot of a purple flower (Antonia regretted not being able to photograph it, having forgotten to bring along her camera), and an antique sewing machine upon whose wooden frame rested rusty pieces of sheet metal, which caught Paula's attention.

"Have you seen what they are?" she asked Antonia with a murmur that almost didn't escape her wonder.

Antonia's gaze followed Paula's pointing finger. There atop the sewing machine were two piles of plates that each carried a distinctive sign: engraved on the laminated surfaces of their sectioned nude bellies alternated the unmistakable designs of a penis or vagina.

"Can you believe it, Antón? They're ex-votos, charms," replied Paula dazzled by the discovery.

Antonia picked up several of the laminated figures. They were light, smooth although slightly curved, with a simplicity in the almost childish drawing that resolved the complexity of the sexes in a curve or a simple line: a coin tossed in the air, heads or tails, the doors of destiny opening or closing according to the inevitable design of the restrooms: ladies/gentlemen.

"Young man," broke in the woman at the stall. "Take whatever you like, just don't mix them up."

"Don't worry, ma'am," replied Antonia. "Do you know where they're from?"

"A church that burned down in San Miguel de Allende."

"So they are indeed religious charms," exclaimed Francisco disbelievingly as he finally reached the stall. "Well, after all, if there are charms in the form of a heart, liver, leg, or arm to seek help and cures, I don't see why there wouldn't be charms for impotence, sterility, syphilis, why even AIDS."

"Or to help you define your sexuality…," mused Antonia with a pensive gaze.

"Or to grant you the miracle of opening it, unplugging it," playfully suggested Paula. "I don't know about you two, but I'm buying one."

"Yeah, it's a good idea," replied Antonia, still not choosing between them.

"Don't hesitate," Francisco reiterated. "You better take two…"

"And you don't want some little charm?" Antonia asked him.

Francisco answered categorically, "No, I'm fine the way I am."

Paula and Antonia looked at him and then at each other. It was charming to imagine him without duplicities, ambiguities, blurry lines. Like a boy playing with a spinning top who forgets about the world.

(But Francisco didn't forget everything. As soon as Paula was distracted, looking at some hats, he whispered in Antonia's ear, "Are you going to tell her your secret?"

Antonia seemed not to be listening to him. Carrying the ex-votos that she'd bought wrapped up in a paper bag, she weighed them in her hand and added, "If it were just that simple.")

8

"So women have a penis, it just doesn't emerge from them?" asked Carlos astonished, casting a glance at a print in the book that Paula and Antonia were showing him.

They had at last found a copy of *Humani Corporis Fabrica*, the book by Vesalio they'd been searching for. Months earlier Antonia and Raimundo had found in an anatomy book the fascinating image of a womb that on one extreme recalled the silhouette of a urinal and on the other ended in some lips that looked like glans. By the time Antonia had met Paula she'd almost forgotten about it, but the fact that Paula was a biologist, and that hanging from her office door was a poster with the cover of the book, reminded her of that print. The image on the poster—announcing a symposium on the history of medicine—had been an irresistible lure with that body of a woman dissected amidst a crowd of students and curious onlookers congregated around it to discover its mysteries. It was revealing that a sixteenth century anatomical study had as a front image the uncovered abdomen of a woman, as if by poking among her entrails, resecting muscles and ligaments, could be discovered the secrets of the world...To cut the skin, to perforate, to penetrate... the fascinated gaze of those present, including Vesalio himself who was also represented in kind of a spectacle at once ingenious and macabre: the theater of the inert body. And a retinue of the silhouettes of all those men converted into the shadows of a voracious desire...Antonia could understand them: a similar passion had led her to prod, in her own way, into the mystery of the penis.

"So women have a penis, it just doesn't emerge from them?" The question hung in the air a few moments. They were gathered at the pilot's apartment, where they'd been invited for breakfast that Sunday morning.

"That's what Galeno thought," Paula finally responded, not for nothing the only one there with specific knowledge of the topic, "and it seems Vesalio himself as well, no matter how hard he tried to base his investigations on the direct observation of cadavers: they used to believe that women were a kind of inside-out sock of men... That's why this print, however much it represents a sectioned uterus in the upper part, ends with that sort of glans at the bottom."

"But seen as a whole," Antonia ventured, "apart from the incredible similarity that the uterus shares with a urinal and a penis, the print can also be read as a kind of fantasy of ambiguity."

Paula and Carlos turned to look at Antonia, who had no recourse but to explain.

"Come on, it's appealing to imagine oneself on the edge of things or to think that things don't have to be so cut and dried: male/female, black/white, good/bad..."

"And if Raimundo were here," chimed in Carlos, "for sure he'd tell us, 'Neither light nor darkness, but shadow...'"

"Don't kid around..."

"But things are indeed cut and dried," added Paula, "at least in a classificatory principle. Did you know that the Latin word *sexus* has the same origins as cut, separate, section? Over here the women's room, over there the men's..."

"Well, in New York, Paris, London," said Carlos giving the book back to Antonia, "even right here in a few bars in Condesa, there are restrooms that both men and women can use...That's to say, you can't even take a piss with pleasure any more just among your peers."

"Because the difference aren't so cut and dried," Antonia said, casting a complicit gaze at Paula. "There are those who try to obviate them. But neither is it a matter of saying they don't exist: for example, the urinal…"

"Or tampons," reflected Paula humorously. "And on that note, Antón, haven't I told you that a friend of mine who's just arrived from England was saying that over there women are already using urinals? They put on some plastic contraption and pee standing up."

"The *clochardes* who pee in the Seine do all right standing on their feet. So?"

Paula and Carlos gazed at Antonia, as if the fact of tracing Vesalio's book and such a fascination for urinals forced him to have an answer. Antonia remained silent a few moments: she perceived a terrain more vast and undetermined, a kind of changing nebulosity whose sign had more to do with the question than the assertion.

"Desire…," she stammered, observing the cover of Vesalio's book with the woman dissected and the pack of men avid for knowledge. "Isn't it desire that truly makes us sexual? What or who attracts you? Tell me what you desire and I'll tell you who you are…"

"Or tell me *whom* you desire and I'll tell you what you are," said Paula, slipping the words in as if she were trying to pass a little rolled up message through a crack in a massive wall. "In the terrain of desire it doesn't seem that equal relations exist. It's always a matter of a subject and an object, but…who? which?"

"Seems like a tongue twister, a labyrinth of words," mused Carlos.

"It is…and also a labyrinth of feelings," added Antonia pensively.

9

Ever since she was a little girl, Antonia had read about the fickleness of the Greek gods and their metamorphoses. She had been dazzled by the imminence of a mystery, the absolute will of a Zeus transformed into golden rain, a bull, a swan, an eagle, in order to possess an imprisoned princess as much as some bashful youth: stories about how the gods could be human in their passions. As a girl she didn't realize it, but in each story—she now thought—pulsed desire. It frightened her to consider that though they seemed like children's stories or invented fables, still some same vigor, a steeled fever, loomed behind them: vast dominions of desire and a power that works in the shadows.

June was approaching and with it the great flowering of magnolias and her twenty-eighth birthday. Francisco gave Antonia a copy of Ovid's *Metamorphoses* illustrated with works of art. She read it passionately: there was the treasure of stories that she had known in the form of fairy tales and mythologies when she was a little girl. She was surprised at how many stories she knew, including the one about the offspring of Aphrodite and Hermes who in one sole body was melded both young man and maiden, and about whom, contrary to what one might think, she took no great interest. On the other hand the fable about Tiresias, who being a man was suddenly transformed into a woman, didn't cease to surprise him. Like him, Antonia had also known pleasure as both sexes but was far from considering one better than the other. In any case, pleasure had always emerged in function of who was awakening her desire. Observing the eagle in a feverish whirlwind that carried off a fearful Ganymede in a painting by Peter Paul Rubens, she imagined an invisible and more powerful claw soaring off with them in tow towards the momentary chasm that is every passion.

And she thought of Paula—how much longer would that moment last for them?

10

She had forgotten to take the urinal back from Raimundo's studio. Because Antonia knew that "forget" wasn't the exact word, she headed to the photographer's apartment without knowing if in the end she would haul the urinal home. Before leaving on a business trip that was going to last two or three weeks—taking photos of the state of Yucatán for a tourism guide—Raimundo left her the keys to his place. "I don't understand you," he had scolded before leaving. "You're crazy about urinals, I give you one and you don't even take pictures of it…Well, do whatever you want."

It was no longer atop the pedestal in the living room. She found the urinal in the room with Raimundo's altar, covered by a piece of black velvet, converted into the shadow of itself. To see it hidden in a corner like the Minotaurinal at the Civil Registrar that she had visited with Malva, in that shadowy room where an image of the Souls in Purgatory presided over the photographer's devotion, revived her interest. She placed it in the center of the room, lit the candles on the altar, brought over a couple of lamps, took out her camera and proceeded to deflower it.

In every possible angle, poking into its luminous and reflective material, accentuating the profiles and contrasts, one shot after another, with a fever that led her to violate its resplendent skin, Antonia found herself practicing a kind of dissection, a loving anatomical study, a siege to seize the silent moan lost in the dark opening of a nameless murmur. Suddenly she stopped. She would never grasp it all. Even with its legs wide open, unabashedly showing its secrets, it still resisted her. Fortunately. She exhaled comfortably and only then began to shoot the camera.

She finished all her rolls of film. In the end the urinal yawned exhausted and happily drifted off to sleep. Antonia covered it with the velvet cloth again and shut off the lights, not pausing to look at the prayer of the shadows winding around the base of the image of the Souls, which she had committed so much to memory that she had forgotten it. And she left the room without making a sound, smiling, tiptoeing so not to wake himself.

11

If man was the dream of a shadow, what was the shadow like that had dreamt of Paula, who now slept there after making love? Her naked body was a broad smile—did the shadow then smile and they communicate in dreams? Sitting on a small chair a few steps from the bed, Antonia—naked, too—contemplated them, her legs crossed as if the bulge between them weren't a hindrance. It wasn't the first time that she'd observed Paula sleeping: besides the calm the sight instilled, she marveled at not tiring of looking at her. This time, however, something else happened. Afternoon was fading and a ray of light passed at an angle through the window towards the woman's belly. She must have felt a pleasurable warmth because she immediately changed position and opened her legs. The light fell now upon the lock of her sex: surprised, prying, that light asked with subtle knocks, "What lies behind this?"

Antonia, who had never before so contemplated a vagina, not even as a woman, and who now at every moment pondered the undeniable materiality of her penis, finally noticed carefully the hidden horizon that a simple fold, a line barely drawn, insinuated.

And she was left disarmed, astonished, enraptured: the lock held the gaze with the promise to reveal its mystery at one moment or another—that is, with the certainty of always hiding its secret.

(But isn't it like that with every human being? wondered Antonia after recovering from the enchantment and could divert her gaze a bit. Doesn't the same thing happen to every person beyond the palpable evidence of a pound of flesh or a cut's uncertain hint? Who doesn't have secrets? And above all, who knows all of those about oneself? Antonia could have continued with other questions, such as, Who is an open book? Who isn't a labyrinth, a questioner, an undefined penumbra, a desire, a shadow? But at that moment in which she still evaded the reflective gaze of Paula's vagina, she discovered someone else observing him: in the corner a full-length mirror with a pointed arch-like shape captured a few of the room's elements: the outline of the girl's body, her brilliant gaze—Paula had awakened and in the mirror watched him watching her—and the silhouette of Antonia herself in profile against the retreating light. Then on the mirror's surface their gazes tenuously, lovingly kissed. Antonia thought it was like contemplating oneself inside a painting, a photo or a dream whose borders were fading, were melting into a revealing transparency: they were both shadows now lit not only by desire but—Antonia hesitated—love?)

12

"So was love next?" Antonia asked herself while Paula was bathing and she stood yet before the empty bed and the oval mirror. Before leaving the room Paula had turned on a light, and thus Antonia could still observe herself, although outside night had fallen. The truth is she was pleased with himself and couldn't help but recognize a freshness, a breeze despite all the strong winds. And, more than anything else, she liked that. Even more than that her body had maintained an uncertain limit, a restrained sensuality that, she had to admit, delighted her. Something similar was happening to her with Paula: to feel her elastic, like living water molding itself to the continents, running through the fissures. Antonia noticed then that her member, asleep just a few seconds earlier, was stretching with its arms out. It was one of the ten or twelve daily erections that made him aware of himself. She tenderly caressed it: it was part of her body and he was now what he was because of that body: it felt like a tailor-made suit, but she didn't cease to perceive herself behind it. Behind: a crevice, a waterfall, a balloon, a feather, a pebble. Antonia shook her head at such a range of wild associations. She was happy and bubbling, for the first time unworried about the future. She raised her hand in the mirror and greeted her shadow.

13

"Is that what the desire of men is like?" asked Antonia looking Francisco straight in the face. They'd just closed the bookstall and the boxes rested on the sidewalk, waiting to be loaded into the car trunk.

Antonia had confided to him her latest experiences with Paula—the fling with Raimundo, of course she kept to herself—and now tossed out a question that in reality confirmed her astonishment.

Once they'd put all the boxes in the car, Francisco invited her to take a walk. A recent drizzle had polished the street and the night air was cool and quiet. The traffic of cars and pedestrians was thinning, so that the city became a passable space and Antonia readily accepted the offer. They walked a couple of blocks before Francisco picked up their conversation from a few minutes earlier.

"You were asking me whether that's what the desire of men is like, like your desire for Paula that has led you to discover so many hidden corners, so many folds and I don't know how many other things. Look, Antón, I'm going to sound cutting and even rude, but this is what I truly think. The desire in men is like the train in that Jon Voight movie, remember?, I think it was called *Runaway Train*...I mean," and his hands simulated the space of a moving tunnel that embraced the dimensions of his face, "that's what the desire of men is like, a unidirectional movement forward, with no going back. And nothing more."

Antonia cracked a smile: yes, she'd already noticed that kind of rapid train in full escape.

"And forgive me for what I'm going to say now, but I've thought it since the first time I saw how crazy you were about urinals." Francisco stopped and put his hand on Antonia's shoulder. "All that story, Antón, about the desire of men, that thing about urinals being something more than just urinals, are only women's fantasies. We men are much simpler than that...I'd even say rudimentary..."

Water Everywhere

1

A flowering pubis is a gaze that strips you, Antonia thought, while shaving Paula's sex before taking some photos in Raimundo's studio. Before her transformation, she never would have thought either of feeling attracted to the enigma of a pubis or contemplating it uncovered.

The truth is that it all began as a game: Paula swearing that she'd never let herself be touched and Antonia seducing her with a whispered phrase unfamiliar even to herself, "I want your little girl's pussy," and Paula repeating "no," but already not so forcefully, showing herself again as an adolescent, almost pubescent, almost light, smiling because the illusion of so imaging herself swirled within.

It was finally Paula who asked to be depilated when Antonia was already content just to take pictures of her with a magnolia bud she'd managed to find thanks to a seller of exotic flowers at the Jamaica market. Vigilant, the urinal Raimundo had given her observed the scene. Despite its pretended indifference, it seemed to smile when Antonia put the magnolia bud within it before leaving the room. It wasn't more than a couple of minutes before she came back with a pair of scissors, shaving cream and a razor and dedicated herself to shaving Paula as if she were pruning a flower garden: carefully, uncompromisingly. Quite soon the pubis of Paula emerged whitely as if she were ten again. Antonia contemplated it in all its transparency: a tender and luminous gaze that laid bare still nameless desires.

Moved by the wonder that a razor could reveal, Paula asked if she could look at herself in a mirror. Antonia brought one from Raimundo's bedroom and placed it before her. They smiled at each other, once again complicit.

"You see...I've never raped a little girl," said Antonia before starting to kiss her.

(But at the moment Paula yielded, Antonia perceived the urinal moving, as if it had finally awakened from its shadowy dream to signal her: inside it, the magnolia bud had opened in full its petals and begun to exhale its tart and penetrating aroma.

"I used to be a woman," Antonia also exhaled definitively and unstoppably.)

2

What does one do in the face of mystery? One accepts it...or rejects it. Of course, one can look for explanations. Recalling a specialized magazine she'd recently looked over at the institute, Paula could have asked: if it had happened to Alexina Barbin in 1860, an extraordinary case of hermaphroditism, like so many others that had remained in the shadows if not for her memoirs being found and published by Michel Foucault in 1978, *why couldn't that be the

---

*These memoirs were accompanied by medical reports and newspaper articles from the time under the title *Herculine Barbin, dite Alexine B*, Paris: Gallimard, 1978. The title of the English translation is more descriptive: *Herculine Barbin: Being the Recently Discovered Memoirs of a Nineteenth Century French Hermaphrodite*, prologue by Michel Foucault, translation by Richard McDougal, New York: Pantheon Books, 1980. After a civil case tried in 1860, Alexina was known by the name Abel Barbin until committing suicide in 1868.

scientific explanation for what had happened to Antón, which was what Paula called Antonia, even in her dreams? She could have also seized on the argument of surgical intervention, recalling for example that although more complex and prolonged than that of men—around twelve hours, according to what she'd heard on a television news report—a kind of constructive surgery could add to women who needed it that desired missing pound of flesh, even if the lack of feeling in the created area only reinforced the immense power of the fantasy...Then we should ask whether Antón had been operated on in order to incarnate his greatest phantom, although at the risk of not feeling anything...

Paula was a biologist and any of these questions or rationalizations would have been forgiven. Instead, despite the astonishment, the uncertainty, the stammering logic that was opening itself up, she remained silent and hugged Antonia.

(But there are always fissures. It wasn't true that one could only accept or reject mystery. As well exists the state of suspension: the wake of removed particles, in a diffuse and perplexed movement, which will end up settling sooner or later. Paula kept silent that day and the following. After more than a week had passed she informed Antonia that her trip to Italy had been moved up. Didn't Antonia recall that research project comparing Popo and Stromboli that she had talked about when they'd first met? She was going to travel to the Aeolian Islands. It was a done deal. To Antonia's silence, Paula added on the phone, "Don't be sad. It's only for the summer." But when they finally said goodbye at the airport, neither knew what the future held.)

3

Antonia was in a café waiting for Francisco to arrive. His voice on the phone had sounded more nervous than normal: they must see each other urgently. While she waited, looking through the window at the avenue before her, Antonia noticed a couple pushing a stroller who, after hesitating where to sit, ended up at one of the outside tables just in front of her own. They seemed to get along well: she busied herself fixing the baby's little hat on his head, looked over the menu, and suggested to her husband what to have; he hesitated but let himself be convinced and finally, his chest as stiff as if he were reciting lines in a play, gave both their orders to the waiter who had come over to the table. The woman looked at him gratefully and, smiling, straightened his shirt collar, which was apparently out of place. The baby played with a rattle attached by a ribbon to the awning of the blue stroller. The man cast a glance around and breathed with the satisfaction of a little God the Father contemplating the goodness of his kingdom. Antonia, looking at them attentively despite perceiving a rather theatrical air about the situation, a subtly elaborated harmony, wasn't surprised when the woman pointed at a young woman in a miniskirt walking on the sidewalk across the street. They both seemed to disapprove connivingly of her attire, perhaps not so much for the shortness of the skirt but because of the girl's thin legs. From the woman's strident gestures, Antonia could imagine her saying, "How ridiculous! If she doesn't have anything to show, why is she showing off her scrawny legs?" And the husband nodded, approving of his wife's words; and then took the opportunity, when she bent forward to help straighten up the baby who could no longer reach the rattle and had begun to whimper, to examine the girl's long legs and enjoy them while she stopped at a candy stall, noting how being so firm and limber they promised an expanding pleasure. Back at the table, the woman managed to perceive her husband's desire, that gravitation of the masculine gaze that had turned his attention away from his wife. And just then, while the man composed himself and was thankful that the waiter had arrived with the sodas and ice cream at precisely the right moment, Antonia could see, while the disenchantment shone briefly in the woman's eyes, that perfect kingdoms are not of this world. They shared their ice creams and smiled again. The pact, that conviction to fill in fissures—or cracks, or chasms—at whatever the cost, had been re-established.

Francisco still hadn't shown up. Returning to the couple she'd been observing, Antonia ventured to think, "Perhaps the matter of the sexes is no more than the coercion of tight clothing..." Alone with her coffee, no one could stop her if she decided to become philosophical or even metaphysical because, surely, she wandered hungry for affection and company. And so she went on: "Nobody knows better than I do how tight gender clothes are...Despite the modernity of our times, the body I-woman continues to be a dress with a corset, the same as the body I-man is a suit of armor. We worry about and concern ourselves with differences (even the body I-gay), but there are gasping fish out of water and deeper lacerations: gaping desire, the anguish of being alive, of solitude, of sadness, finally, in the fact of our going to die, inexorably, without reason. How right are those who say life is an absurd wound," she finished in a low voice at the moment Francisco appeared out of nowhere and took a seat beside her.

"'Is life an absurd wound'? I didn't know you liked the tango," replied Francisco while he pulled the few hairs from a beard still reluctant to grow. "My father loved them, and that's why I too know a few by heart. Although in this case I like the Mexican version better: 'Nothing is life worth, life is worth nothing. One always starts out crying and so crying one always ends...' You haven't heard from Paula, right? Well, I'm afraid I have more bad news. It's about Raimundo. It's been three weeks since anybody has heard from him. He left the team of tourism guides in Playa del Carmen and went to photograph cenotes. Knowing him, he's capable of disappearing for weeks or even months...The problem is someone else from the group vacationing in the area found his camera, that Leica he carried everywhere, in a flea market in Chetumal..."

"And how are you sure it's his camera?" asked Antonia, trying to avail herself of anything she could.

Francisco pressed his lips together before responding, "It had a half-taken roll of film in it, nothing but photos of shadows and ghostly silhouettes..."

4

Once again in the labyrinth. She didn't know how—after wandering around with neither sense nor direction, the idea of hanging onto the walls already forgotten, since more than a wish to escape, a concealed and inexplicable desire pushed her forward—but she arrived to the offices of the Civil Registrar that she had once visited with Malva. She carried the camera strap over her shoulder, so it couldn't have been chance that guided her steps there. She had to see the Minotaurinal. Photograph it. While she was waiting for an opportunity to sneak into the women's room—why the hell were there so many people doing business that day?—she stroked the possibility of stripping it bare, of breaking its binds and knowing its walled-over secrets. The truth is she'd been thinking about the process for a time, an incision with a razor blade—or at least with the point of a pen, she needed to find a pen—in the plastic surface enveloping it, and then, with all her feelings right on the edge, jumping to the laceration, the happy violence of opening and unveiling. And to do so step by step, to register each moment with the eye of the camera, to capture the grade of light and shadow emitted by the object and trap its refulgent trace in the sensitive skin of the film...To take ownership of the object, to devour it, to embody it.

A boy wearing a janitor's uniform and pushing a garbage can on wheels approached the restrooms. Antonia hurried to catch up with him before he turned the corner down the hallway, and without thinking twice asked his help, arguing it concerned a report on the cleanliness of women's public restrooms. With a gaze at once sly and distrustful, the young man refused. Although they were in a corner hidden from the view of the main hallway, Antonia discretely slipped a few pesos into his pocket. He took a quick look around and said, "Just five minutes," letting Antonia by before putting the garbage can in front of the door so no one else could enter.

As soon as Antonia crossed the threshold, it seemed a different place than the one she'd seen with Malva. Opaque, lit by a fluorescent light that clouded the view, Antonia thought the emptiness was a dream. It hadn't occurred to her that someone might have removed her Minotaurinal. She blamed herself for not having shot it earlier, and a feeling of nausea began to float in the pit of her stomach, when her eyes finally found the bulk she had fantasized about so many times. She ran towards it and touched the face hidden by the plastic bag.

She'd found a pen and could free it and so hear its voice and its answers. But the bag, tightly encircling the object's curves and edges, couldn't silence the obscure seduction of her nameless desire. On the contrary, masking it only made its disquieting beauty even more obvious.

She noticed a crack in the mosaic wall that she hadn't seen before, which descended over the Minotaurinal like a bolt of lightning pointing at a mystery. She didn't dare rip the enigma, nor alter its sleepless, transparent veiling. She just opened the aperture of the lens as wide as possible and took one photo, without a flash and without taking a breath.

5

Not long afterwards they heard from Raimundo. Yes, his camera had been stolen but he wasn't worried about it. In a town near Chichén Itzá he'd met María, a school teacher who had brought some kids on a summer school course to visit the Mayan archeological site. As soon as he saw her—a radiant luminosity in her eyes, the friendly way in which she addressed the group of teenagers, the simple dignity of walking as if she knew with certainty her place in the world—the photographer knew he had to follow and meet her. Of course, there was also the attraction of the cenotes, which forced him to find a waterproof camera so that he could record the luminous penumbra of that kind of marine well where the exterior light, coming at times through the small throat of a cave, fell in a cascade that hit the subterranean water, turning it into a limbo where the submerged bodies and objects acquired an immaterial transparency. A sort of luminous Penumbria.

And all that he'd told Antonia over the phone, announcing that he was returning soon but only to take care of a few things before heading back to the Yucatán. Although, of course, the easiest thing would be if María agreed to come with him to Mexico City…

"So you've fallen in love?" asked Antonia moved by the news from her friend.

After a pause, Raimundo answered through a loud laugh,

"That's what they want you to think…But yes, everything would seem to indicate that yes, I've been caught…And you, how are things going with Paula?"

"Good. So good that she's in the Aeolian Islands now, been there three weeks and I still haven't heard from her."

"Then have you broken up? But you got along so well…"

"Well, that's what we wanted you to think," joked Antonia. "But I'll tell you all about it later. When are you coming back?"

6

"What can I tell you, Antón? Your Minotaurinal seems a marvel to me," said Raimundo, holding the photo print that Antonia had brought him, his face filled with amazement. "It really is extraordinary, above all for the fact they've wrapped it up like that to make it less conspicuous, but being covered up in the women's bathroom makes it even more provocative. It seems as if the covering was in reality to prevent some woman—whether out of curiosity, ignorance or perversion—from using it. You've photographed a jewel. Moreover, I'm sure the person who took the initiative to cover it was a man, perhaps deep down in order to hide his own sex in the women's room. It would be interesting to know what a woman would have done."

Antonia remained silent, but a smile twisted on her lips while she looked at the photo of the Minotaurinal and listened to her friend's enthusiastic words.

"It's curious. Right before coming back we met in a bar some friends of María, Sophie and Rodrigo, foreigners who live there. She's French and he's Chilean. We really hit it off, they had a refined sense of humor, I suppose that's why they get along so well with

María...Well, after eating and talking and already a bit drunk, Sophie had to go to the restroom. But there was a line of women and without a second thought she went into the men's room. The two guys in there ran out furious and one even went to complain to the manager. Sophie came back dying of laughter and told us everything. She was amused by the reaction of the Latin Americans because in Paris discos, when there aren't unisex bathrooms, women are used to going in the men's room instead of waiting and nobody makes a face or a comment. I suppose she wounded the pride of Rodrigo, who, no wonder is Chilean, because he immediately attacked the Parisians for only pretending not to react, while in reality it's an invasion of privacy and in fact there are a lot of men who don't like to pee next to other men, much less in front of a woman. And to make things even, one would have to see if Sophia would like some unknown man watching her pee...To make a long story short, we got tangled up in a discussion about whether there should be restrooms for just one sex. I, of course, spoke in favor of preserving the right to life of that rare and beautiful animal in danger of extinction: the urinal. María backed me up: in her opinion there should not only be more and better public urinals, but they should even be in private homes (she knows well the urgencies of her thirteen-year-old son who runs to the bathroom, yanks up the lid, making it fall and bounce, and then sprays all over, getting everything wet...) As you can see, Antón, there's more than enough cloth to cut from if you decide that you want to organize a book around the theme, or if you've thought about mounting an exhibit of the photos you've taken...Although I can already imagine the reaction of a lot of people—more than one person will be scandalized. Marvelous, no?"

Antonia nodded. She took back the image of the Minotaurinal and put it in the portfolio where she kept the other pictures of urinals she had been collecting. "The matter of the urinals, of the sexes, of identity…if it doesn't scandalize you at least it gets your guard up. It's an obscure affair—a lot of things move around in the shadows, you know? And suddenly people choose to take shelter, or to take off…"

"Any relation to a Melusina named Paula?"

Antonia didn't answer. Another time her eyes might have filled with tears: had she learned to suppress her emotions like a good little boy, or rather had she ended up accepting Paula's silence as another form of mystery, that consisting of the relation and chemistry of beings that charge things with a sense of themselves, and in face of which it's not worth the trouble of wasting time on reasons and explanations?

"Doesn't it seem, Antón, that when we love we become shadows, ghosts of a desire we believe to be our own, but which in reality don't belong to us? I think I already told you that we men are the fantasy of women's desire. First of all, it's always a woman who writes her messages of love or discouragement on our bodies. We are books written by feminine hands. María now writes upon me and despite knowing that writing always leads to silence, I can't help but put myself in her hands. That's why I'm going back to the Yucatán next week. You should come along, even just for a couple of days. Think about it. María would be happy to meet you. I've told her about you and of course the other guys, too."

7

Why did Raimundo think that men were the fantasy of women's desire? Where had he gotten the idea that as well they were books written by feminine hands? After talking to Antonia, Carlos scoffed at the idea.

"What's going on," pointed out the pilot in a restaurant where they'd just finished eating one Saturday morning, "is that Raimundo lends too much importance to the famous feminine mystique, as if the secret of creation and origin of the world resided in women... He's surely one of those men who even envies getting pregnant and giving birth."

"Yeah, he told me that the other day," confessed Antonia.

"Well, that doesn't surprise me, nor would it to learn he'd like to wake up some day and have a vagina instead of a penis. Now I'm not saying he's a fag. Let me explain: I've told you about Alexis, my Alexis, right? Well, my Alexis would confess to you that he also has wished that and not because he's a repressed homosexual but for the simple desire to know what women feel. I suppose it might be helpful to menstruate to understand them better. Although I can already hear Matatías answering, 'You'd have to be a little queer just to accept the idea of them sticking it in you instead of you doing the penetrating.'"

"I agree," said Francisco sitting down at the table with them. "Sorry I'm late. I see you already ate. May I know who was getting eaten alive?"

"Your friend the photographer," said Carlos as he took out a cigarette for a smoke. He held out the pack to the others, who declined, and asked the waiter for coffee.

"Well, as for Raimundo," added the new arrival, "I refrain from offering an opinion. It's already happened that he could convince me of anything. So, is he coming today?"

"No," replied Carlos. "He's quite busy with his new amorous and photographic project. He's returning to Yucatán..."

"Yeah," Antonia assented. "He's gone after the shadow of his desire."

A dark, beautiful woman wearing a very tight dress entered the café in company of an older man. Without indicating to each other to do so, attracted by the magnetism of that rotund body, the three friends followed her in a long breathless gaze.

"Did you see that?" Carlos finally asked when the couple had disappeared in the back of the establishment. "The shadow of desire, you were saying, Antón? I think we just saw its radiant incarnation."

Antonia agreed with a deep sigh that caught Francisco's attention. At that moment Carlos got up to go to the men's room and Francisco confronted her.

"I never imagined myself sharing these events with you," he said. "Any news from Paula?"

Antonia shook her head no.

Francisco patted her lightly on the shoulder before adding, "Cheer up...that's what the heart is for: to use it up while you can."

8

A long distance call, the voice arrived in waves crashing against her reefs. The heart, Paula had spoken of her heart. Did she mention chimeras, or did Antonia only imagine it between the tumult of words and emotions that rose gigantically and broke in the crashing of desires, flowering, unhealing wounds fluttering like sea foam? Amidst her confusion, Antonia had rescued a polished piece of wood from the shipwreck: "Why don't you meet me in Lipari?" And without thinking about it, Antonia said yes. Yes, a big yes, opening her arms to the miracle.

9

"More than in the body, secrets and indifference reside in the heart. The true sex and authentic identity open the way from within. The rest of it is just apparel, vestments, costumes. It takes a lot of work to go naked, with the heart exposed..." Antonia was surprised to hear Raimundo's words confirming that the photographer knew her secret. She had gone looking for him to recount Paula's phone call.

"Have you known for a long time?" asked Antonia, feeling the dizziness just starting.

"Not from the beginning. But later I figured it out by your fascination with urinals. Only a woman could look at them like you do, discerning the hunger of desire, our absolute sex, that which leaves us craving, stupefied, our true mystery for which the essential isn't in the answer, but in its interrogating gaze: 'Only the question remembers,' wrote the poet Edmund Jabès. Do you know his work?"

"No, I don't. But he's right: only the question replies," Antonia ventured to paraphrase, remembering the veiled face of the Minotaurinal.

10

Before leaving for Yucatán, Raimundo gave Antonia a gift. His taxi was about to arrive, so he spoke quickly. "I don't like goodbyes. But since you're leaving, too, and who knows when we'll see each other again, I had to give this to you. One favor, though: don't open it until I've left. You'll see the definition isn't very good, but as there wasn't much time, poor Paul, a designer friend of mine who helped me bring the idea to fruition, had to work miracles."

135

Antonia took the portfolio the photographer held out with a smile.

"Well, thank you very much. Really, can't I help you with your suitcase or camera gear?"

But Raimundo was already walking towards the elevator, used to carrying all his own baggage.

"Just one thing," he said, holding the elevator door open with a leg. "Take care of yourself, eh? And if for whatever reason you don't come back soon, we'll see each other at Carnival in Venice, OK?"

"Or we'll see each other on the banks of a cenote, who knows."

The elevator doors closed. Antonia stood at the window to watch the rushing Raimundo, who after putting his suitcases inside the taxi took time to look up and give a brief wave.

She remained looking at the street and made out in the distance a pair of flowering magnolia trees. Would she find magnolias in Italy? She was in a hurry. That morning she had to apply for a new passport—of course, confronting the complexities that act might result in made her dizzy—buy a plane ticket, exchange money. She was leaving the apartment when she came across on the table the portfolio Raimundo had given her. She went to the window seeking better light and opened it. A beautiful image: from the paper emerged a girl with a childlike pubis, completely naked…and bountiful as a fountain, which Antonia recalled having seen before. Only there was a unique difference in Raimundo's: instead of the pitcher the girl had carried upon her shoulder, which she spilled with a gesture of absolute surrender, there appeared an object familiar to Antonia: Duchamp's pristine urinal emptying out as well with an unstoppable innocence. The image was so beautiful that it took her quite a while to notice the message written at the bottom in Raimundo Ventura's swift handwriting:

> For Antonia, who was able to look
> at the same fountain in a different way.

11

She was used to wearing her hair tied in a ponytail, but that day decided to let it hang loose. And like the first time she went out after her transformation—how could she forget—she put on the most casual clothes: a white shirt, a light jacket, and loafers. Before leaving the apartment, she looked at herself in the mirror. She was undoubtedly Antonia, but would those who didn't know her—and who would have to vouch for her legal identity—recognize him?

Now that she was waiting her turn to submit the application at the office of Foreign Relations, she couldn't stop imagining what might happen. To start out with, indefinitely pushing back her trip, being submitted to questioning, perhaps a trial, or even jail…No, better to avoid such ideas and not run headlong into uncertainty. All things considered, beyond such simulacra, masks or mirages, she continued being who she was. Would these bureaucrats understand that identity begins beneath the skin? In whatever form, she had decided to confront what might come, but if she didn't have to take out her pike—smiling to recall that it had been a long time since she'd thought about armor—much, much better.

Her turn arrived. She walked firmly to the counter. The man who took the papers observed her a few moments before verifying the information and looking over the previous passport. Antonia had kept herself just close enough to that limiting identity which depending upon the eyes looking could tip the balance. But would it be enough now? All the man did was take her finger prints and say politely to come back later for the new passport. Just like that, nothing more, no objection or request for any explanation.

12

Instead of the picture of a fan and a pipe—or their variations: from the elaborate silhouette of a lady with a hoopskirt and a man in a top hat to the minimalist figures that resolved the difference by the width of the hips—Antonia stumbled upon a pair of unusual signs:

Cappuccino/Espresso

What did this imply? She peeked into both restrooms. In neither one was there a urinal. (Is that why Raimundo had spoken of a species on the verge of extinction?) She looked at the doors again and hesitated. So Paula was right that "sex" and "to section" had a common origin: only for that purpose did oppositions seem useful: to simplify, to avoid confusions and uncertainties. But here, a coffee shop near the offices of the Ministry of Foreign Relations where she'd gone after the passport scare, the restrooms playfully suggested a slight gradation, a modulation in the amount of coffee, very much with the tone of the place. Of course there were people—like the older woman now asking permission to get by—who became annoyed because it made them hesitate and…decide.

The woman ended up going into the restroom marked "Cappuccino" and Antonia shrugged her shoulders before crossing the threshold of the one marked "Espresso." While she easily undid her pants and took out her penis in the twinkling of an eye, taking care in good humor that Newton's Fifth Law of Displacement didn't make her spill too many drops out of place, Antonia thought how the distinction between those two doors that had represented the destiny of Western mankind, at least since there had been restrooms, not only became blurred (as in the present situation) but on occasion—like in the case of unisex restrooms and their single door—turn out to be non-existent...But the more one wanted to obviate the differences—because, clearly, who is only a man in the body of a man or uniquely a woman in the body of a woman?— there still remained unquestionable differences. Looking closely at the matter, not many for sure, but an undeniable one that very few people paid attention to: the act of urinating.

Just after Antonia came out of the restroom and sat down at the table, the waiter approached to ask if she wanted anything else.

"A cappuccino? An espresso?" insisted the man.

"How about a latte...just for a change," smiled Antonia.

13

He or she—because there was room for doubt about the gender, although it mattered little for those who could perceive the indifferent beauty—landed at the airport in Lipari, the biggest of the Aeolian Islands, at noon one day in June. The trip had taken more than eighteen hours due to the connections and Antonia felt exhausted. While contemplating the archipelago and the blue immensity through the plane window, she suddenly felt fear, stubborn and suffocating. She had traveled all the way to this corner of the world to find a woman and now she felt afraid. Had she done the right thing? The doubt grew as they got off the plane and she walked with the other passengers towards the exit. She turned into the restroom. The faces of the urinals were like many others she had seen before and this calmed her a bit. Everywhere life had folded, like the sea to its shores.

Antonia also had to fold, although for different purposes. Hidden aims, a hand in the shadow tracing the way. And if after trying Paula ended up rejecting her? She went out to the promenade again but didn't have the strength to go any further. How she missed her friends, including Carlos, who surely would have said, "To travel so far only to have doubts at the last second. See what a fag you are…" Then she remembered Francisco when they'd said goodbye at the airport. "Be sure to write," he said with a hug. When they separated, Antonia's eyes were shining and Francisco reproached her, "No tears. As Raimundo would say, trust your shadow and don't look back." And like someone who jumps into the void or dives into the open sea, she decided to jump in and not look back.

14

She'd traveled all the way to the Aeolians to look for a woman, but quickly discovered that in reality she'd gone in search of himself. It wasn't the isle of Crete, certainly not very far away and in whose labyrinth had lived the legendary Minotaur, but rather another mythic setting: the rustic place where Aeolus blew among the islands with an unparalleled force in order to kindle the fire of Vulcan, blacksmith of the gods, in whose honor one of the islands was named. From its volcanic forge in other times had surged the helmet of Athena, the sword of Achilles, the rays of Zeus. But now it was extinguished. Only from Stromboli, the most boreal island of the group, did the divine fire continue to spill out in a serpentine, luminous tail that day and night nourished the sea. She contemplated it aboard a sailboat with Paula, who had made time to accompany Antonia on the trip despite having to give a talk that same afternoon on advances in her research at the Center of Aeolian Studies. They held hands while admiring the volcano's almost perfect cone, its black sand beach and the little white houses that stood out upon its eastern slope. It was a sunny day and the sea gleamed with a vehement intensity. Aeolus and Vulcan, pacified for the moment, allowed them to reach without any problem the unpopulated island of the lighthouse, which emerged like a gigantic rock, abrupt and savage, in the middle of the sea. "Strombolicchio," said the man steering the boat while he approached a smaller and less steep natural scarp, and then he told them they could jump out.

They'd just climbed the two hundred steps of the staircase constructed by the nearby inhabitants when Antonia had the impression that the island was gently galloping across the sea. She wasn't dizzy, but rather felt a joyful seasickness that made her think of happiness. When the heart was in its right place, it was easy to perceive it in the outer world, the same in that lighthouse victoriously erected and penetrating the immense sky, in Paula who laughed and kissed him and ate some grapes she had held in her lap, in the sea that lovingly girded the land and horizon. She'd have to share all this with Francisco and write him when back in Lipari. And also tell him about the *orinatoio* she had seen a couple of days earlier in company of a few of Paula's Sicilian friends. It was in a rustic tavern near the beach, from whose waters perhaps came that immense gleaming white sea shell that the owner of the place had made use of as a urinal *sui generis*. She'd tell him all about that later, as well as the promise of a urinal in a bar in Palermo that was a waterfall spilling upon a wall of black marble. And of course, she could send him photos.*

---

*In reality it wasn't a marble wall but a mirror that in the place's enveloping penumbra seemed a blinking darkness. As soon as one neared, sinuous rivulets began to rain down upon that darkness in a subtle, unceasing cascade. There in the silvery winking surface Antonia discerned her own image as a fountain, capable of spilling over, of pouring out, of overflowing in that limiting zone which was now a metaphor of her own dripping surrender, of her own recognized and disarmed power.

Meanwhile they began descending, enticed to take a swim while the captain caught a nap. Such was the slow-paced rhythm of life in the Aeolians.

They didn't have bathing suits, so as soon as they saw the man going below deck they took off their clothes as if acting mischievously. At first they played around and swam together, but soon separated from each other. Paula preferred staying close to the isle. Antonia decided to risk diving underwater a bit, drawn by the overwhelming intensity of the waters. It must have been the result of the volcanic bed, the quality of the salt, the depth of the marine crevasse—or perhaps Aeolus was whispering secrets into Vulcan's ear—because definitely the sea's deep blue seemed the call of the chasm, a shining promise, a liquid treasure.

Without diving gear she couldn't go under very far, but attempted to descend as far as possible. She tried several times with all the air her lungs could hold. Suddenly, after no more than a few meters, Antonia found herself surrounded by a vibrating blue immensity. Neither sky above her head, nor the ocean floor beneath her feet: she was floating in the middle of the blue. Water everywhere. She felt part of it. Everything in its place. Perhaps it would be worth it not to come out and instead abandon herself to the tempting certainty of the moment.

15

But her heart resisted. Each heartbeat was a question, a desire to go on: vehement, unstoppable. Despite the labyrinths, the doubts, the uncertainty. When Antonia came up out of the infinitely transparent waters and swam again toward the island, she knew she was a minotaur that had survived. As soon as she came ashore and caught her breath, she looked at her translucent hands and skin as if she had emerged from a basin of photo developers. A shipwrecked body, a shadow at last illuminated.

Acknowledgements

This book sought shelter in the luminous shadow of Virginia Woolf, Marcel Duchamp and Man Ray. José Emilio Pacheco granted permission to work above all with the freedom of the writer to exercise a point of view, and for that reason it is dedicated to him.

In the terrain of a poetics of desire and shadow, the illicit gaze of Carlos Davis, Ricardo Vinós, and Arturo Casares was especially valuable. Artists Paul Aracón and Marco Lamoyi oriented and animated the iconographic metaphors. André Breton, Erica Araiza and W.G. Sebald are to good measure responsible for their inclusion between the lines of the text. Marcela González Durán confided to me the lines of the poet Jabès, which later served as an epigraph to these pages.

The complicity of so many friends in the area of public restrooms was undeniable, and without them the transgression would have only remained a fantasy: Ángel Molina, Mauricio Carrera, Ricardo Cinta, Juan José Giovannini, Luis Camacho, Beatriz Clavel, Ignacio Toscano, Pedro Pablo Martínez, David Lida, Víctor Panameño, Patricio Rubio, Jenny Pulido, Fernando Cobo, Alberto Regalado, Alexis and Paul, Ishtar Cardona and other unknown people who opened the doors to me of a world very rarely visited by the feminine sex.

The words and dreams of Julio Cortázar, Javier Contreras, Max Gonsen, Gustavo Jiménez, Mirian Grunstein, Hélène Cixous, Eduardo Corona, Sandra Lorenzano, Sergio González Rodríguez, Roberto Pliego, José Ricardo Chaves, Antonieta Torres Arias, Ricardo

Baduell, Alejandro Valles, Augusto Garcíarrubio and Robert Bly among others undeserving of neglect allowed me to dive in and float back up—I hope—during my research.

Thanks to the generosity of Lucía García Noriega and Claire Becker I was able to achieve the fabulous feat of visiting the Aeolian Islands for a day and a half.

Joaquín Díez-Canedo Flores and Eduardo Antonio Parra read the manuscript and encouraged its publication, which wouldn't have been possible without the always complicit confidence of Marisol Schulz. Somehow or another, as the saying goes, good consciences—especially those with a good nose—will always seek out the guilty one. That's the way it should be.

Photo and Image Credits

Arturo Casares, p. 18

Ana Clavel, pp. 13, 24, 35, 48, 64, 75 [based upon *Untitled* (1926), by Man Ray; realization by Paul Alarcón], 135 [based upon *La Source* (1856) by J.A.D. Ingres, and Fontaine (1917) by M. Duchamp.; realization by Paul Alarcón]

Gustavo Jiménez, pp. 20, 27

Andrea Vesalio, p. 33 [from Book V, *De Humani Corporis Fabrica* (1543); image courtesy of the Fondo Reservado de la Biblioteca Nacional de México]

Jeroen Voolstra, p. 104 [design by Meike van Schijndel, image courtesy of Bathroom Mania!]

Translator's Acknowledgements

Ana Clavel again let me struggle with her complex work: what better material for a translation than a novel about the transformation from one body to another.

Thanks to Juan Arciniega, whose comments, corrections and suggestions helped me hopefully find an elusive narrative voice. His editing was indispensable.

Lourdes Cué, mi chilanga querida, often put down her power tools or hammer and chisel to explain Mexico City slang.

Finally, my sincere appreciation to the Programa de Apoyo a la Traducción de Obras Mexicanas en Lenguas Extranjeras (Protrad) of the Fondo Nacional para la Cultura y las Artes in Mexico. There generous support made this translation possible.

ALSO FROM ALIFORM

Sarminda: Black Desire in a Field of Gold
José Sarney, translated by Gregory Rabassa
ISBN 978-0-615-16478-6   list $14.95

> *"How I loved this beautiful novel…Sarney revives the gold prospectors of Amapá with a sharp sensibility for ethnographic realism permeated by a powerful lyricism."* —Claude Levi-Strauss

Master of the Sea
José Sarney, translated by Gregory Rabassa
ISBN 0-9707652-7-4 ISBN 978-0-9797652-7-7   list $14.95

> *"In the writing of José Sarney I have discovered the knowledge, the language full of imagery, and above all the deeply human quality of the Brazilian people…*Master of the Sea *is a maritime epic brought to life…A monumental work!"* —Claude Levi-Strauss

> "Master of the Sea *is a magnificent, powerful novel. Sarney has come to join Brazil's finest fiction writers."* —Jorge Amado

> 2006 Book of "Especial Merit," Review of Arts, Literature, Philosophy and the Humanities

> Finalist, 2005 National Translation Prize, American Literary Translators Association

> Finalist, 2005 ForeWord Magazine's Book of the Year, translation category

Afloat Again, Adrift: Three Voyages on the Waters of North America
Andrew Keith
ISBN 0-9707653-8-2 ISBN 9780970765284   list $15.95, illustrated with maps

> "Afloat Again, Adrift *embraces the explorer's spirit. Especially recommended for armchair travelers for the vivid descriptions."* —Midwest Book Review

> *"If you've ever canoed for an afternoon and wondered what it might be like to just keep going, Keith's physical and emotional journeys offer inspiration."* —Minnesota Magazine

Desire and Its Shadow
Ana Clavel
ISBN 0-9707652-5-8 ISBN 9780970765253 list $14.95

"*A magical, terrible, dazzling Mexico…*"—Vuelo (Mexico City)

"*An Alice-Lolita trapped between Wonderland and daily life… magical language…*"—Siempre (Mexico City)

"*Ana Clavel…part of [Mexico's] new literary pack.*"
—Publishers Weekly

Die, Lady,Die
Alejandro López
ISBN 0-9707652-6-6 ISBN 9780970765260 list $12.95

"*A story full of madness that combines Almodóvar with Latin pop, fan clubs, soap operas, and lonely hearts magazines.*" —Página 12 (Buenos Aires)

"*Such is the brutal truth of this dizzying novel: there is no reality beyond that of an alienating mass media.*" —Tres Puntos (Buenos Aires)

Jail
Jesús Zárate, translated by Gregory Rabassa
ISBN 0-9707652-3-1 ISBN 9780970765239 list $14.95

"*In its static setting and absurd slant, Zárate's approach resembles Beckett's* Waiting for Godot, *in its questioning of cruelty and power, Kafka's* Penal Colony…*Zárate's novel is something special, and its arrival in English is a welcome gift.*" —San Francisco Chronicle

"*This amazing novel assumes nothing about freedom; as a consequence,* Jail *gives the idea of freedom a tangibility unparalleled by contemporary discussions of the term.*" —Rain Taxi

Luminous Cities
Eduardo Garcia Aguilar
ISBN 0-9707652-1-5 ISBN 9780970765215 list $16.95, illustrated

"*Juxtaposes scenes of decadence and splendor, vulgarity and exquisiteness, creating a dizzying mosaic of urban life.*" —Américas

149

Magdalena: A Fable of Immortality
Beatriz Escalante
ISBN 0-9707652-9-0 ISBN 9780970765222 list $12.95

> *"A fable of feminine ambition that alludes as well to other genres and traditions: biblical and Borgesian parables, alchemical treatises, fairy tales, and contemporary feminist fiction."* —Delaware Review of Latin American Studies

Mariana
Katherine Vaz
ISBN 0-9707652-9-0 ISBN 9780970765291 list $15.95

> *"Mariana's evocation of life in seventeenth-century Portugal glows with colour...in its lyrical descriptions of ordinary lives transfigured, in its detailing of everyday routines and beliefs, and in its account of spiritual and emotional struggles."* —The Times Literary Supplement (London)

> *"Dialogue and descriptions that transport us to the turbulent Portugal of the seventeenth century..."* —Activa (Portugal)

> *"With intensity and erudition, Katherine Vaz has written about the 'forbidden love' that has long fascinated such brilliant minds as Stendahl, Rilke, and Braque."* —La Vanguardia (Spain)

Mexico Madness: Manifesto for a Disenchanted Generation
Eduardo García Aguilar
ISBN 0-9707652-3-1 ISBN 9780970765208 list $14.95

> *"A scathing, sober, and meticulous examination of what it means to be Latin American...a no-holds barred style of unforgettable writing."* —Midwest Book Review

> *"An intriguing blend of journalistic and stream-of-consciousness styles...offering insights into the consequences of such a dramatically changing world."* —Washington Report on the Hemisphere

Mexico Madness is also available in the original Spanish:
Delirio de San Cristóbal: Manifiesto para una generación desencantada
Eduardo García Aguilar
ISBN 968-7646-63-2 list $16.95

150

My World Is Not of This Kingdom
João de Melo, translated by Gregory Rabassa
ISBN 0-9707652-4-X ISBN 9780970765246   list $15.95

> *"Spectacular...a gem..."* —The Los Angeles Times Book Review

> *"My Kingdom Is Not of This World is a sort of chaotic mythological history of the Azores...an insular society in a brutal but pristine and fantastical setting, an Eden soon to be destroyed by politics and greed."* —Ruminator Review

> *"This is a boiling, shocking story, a baroque impasto rather like the creation of the Azores themselves. Language is applied with a palette knife, not a thin brush."* —Revista (Harvard)

ALIFORM PUBLISHING
LITERATURE OF THE AMERICAS AND THE WORLD

WWW.ALIFORMGROUP.COM

INFORMATION@ALIFORMGROUP.COM